TRACING JAJA

ANTHONY KELLMAN

TRACING JAJA

PEEPAL TREE

First published in Great Britain in 2016
Peepal Tree Press Ltd
17 King's Avenue
Leeds LS6 1QS
England

ISBN13: 9781845232993

Supported using public funding by
ARTS COUNCIL
ENGLAND

CHAPTER ONE

The king arrived on the first day of March, two weeks after an invasion of rats on a St. George plantation prompted an early start to cutting the canes. The rodent assault would slow-up cropping, extend it into the rainy season, affect the sucrose content, and disappoint the Queen.

The Pylades, the steam boat on which the king arrived, sat for a time in Carlisle Bay, but he did not see the island as it slowly grew from an ocean-surrounded speck to an undulating mass of greenness, hills speckled with white houses, royal and coconut palms, and the shingled roofs of the city's coral-stone buildings. He saw none of this because of the ailments that made bed-rest a constant feature of his journey.

He knew he'd arrived only when he heard a loud knocking on the cabin door.

'We're here,' the officer said. 'Come.'

King Jaja rose slowly from the bed, steadying himself on the end of the frame. The officer stepped back into the passageway leaving the door slightly ajar. Jaja put on his black leather sandals and limped over to the peg for his admiral's uniform. Sixteen years earlier, Queen Victoria's consul had presented him with the uniform and an inscribed sword in appreciation of his military assistance during the Ashanti War. He'd rarely worn the uniform but had kept it immaculately clean. As he dressed, he scratched at his body, as if some sorrow lay under his skin that flamed like a burning hut. He seemed to bear a defeat that was more than individual.

The passengers on *The Pylades* now began to board smaller boats to take them to Bridgetown Wharf. When the boat carrying

Jaja pulled up at the wharf-side, the crowd lining the waterfront called out and cheered as they stared at the garb he wore. None had seen a black man dressed like this before. They were filled with questions, bright with pride and an inchoate sense that they were witnessing something about their origins, somewhat tarnished but lambent like the morning light flickering on the glazed wharf water. Their voices merged with the sounds of the sea, dying away from the king's hearing only when his carriage reached the city limit. Instead, the horses's hoofs were constant exclamations in his mind, which itched and flared like his body.

Half an hour later, the vehicle arrived at the gate of the Governor's house. The police officer standing in the white guard shed waved the carriage through. One of the guards got out and walked to the front of the house, to the verandah ringed with brilliant red hibiscus. He rapped the brass knocker on the white door that swung open almost at once. The Governor was expecting him.

The guard said, 'He attracted much attention, Sir. Especially among the common people. They watched his every movement, crowded about the carriage, much to our discomfort.'

Governor Sendall had assumed personal oversight for all the details of the king's detention and had arranged the Sunday dawn arrival to avoid the risk of the public spectacle that a Saturday arrival would involve. The authorities had made that mistake in St. Vincent where Jaja had been detained for nearly three years before his transfer to Barbados. He'd arrived in Kingstown Bay around noon when the markets were crowded with people. When news of his arrival reached them, they'd abandoned their buying or selling and flocked to get a glimpse of the king. Because of the pandemonium, the authorities had been forced to keep Jaja and his son Sunday on board the *Icarus* for another day.

The Governor looked away from the guard and out across the gardens, his glance settling on a row of mahoganies. Even with the precautions taken, Jaja's coming had evidently caught the attention of Bridgetown's rabble and word had spread.

'How is he?'

The guard withdrew a thick string-bound document from the leather bag and handed it to the Governor. 'Documents from St. Vincent, Sir. Including reports on his health.'

When Sendall finished scanning the documents, creases appeared on his brow. He pursed his lips and then released them. 'You'd better get him settled in at Two Mile Hill. When he's rested and feeling better, I'll have you bring him over for a visit.' He looked towards the carriage but could see only the right elbow of the other guard and the head of its driver.

The carriage moved out past flamboyants budding red, rows of variegated immortelles, hibiscus courted by yellow butterflies, and sisal lances exclaiming like Jaja's thoughts. It passed through the gate and made the right turn up Two Mile Hill. The carriage, an English Victoria, was stylish, fashionable, all black except for the olive-coloured upholstery, with full suspension springs. The body had been elegantly finished by Thorn of Norwich. Its collapsible hood, when fully extended, covered the entire seating area and two brass lamps hung on each side of the driver's seat like closed eyes. It had been hired from George Whitfield, owner of the Central Ice House on Roebuck Street.

Jaja recalled his sojourn in St. Vincent: the crowds of people who looked like him on the quayside and their thunderous cheers as his carriage was rapidly driven away; the humiliating condescension of the administrator, Robert Llewelyn; the depressing conditions of the Captain's Quarters on the windy promontory at Fort Charlotte; the rented house on Egmont Street next to the public offices; the policemen always on guard, keeping the curious labouring classes at bay; another policeman accompanying him wherever he ventured from home; the place he'd been moved to on Upper Bay Street near the wharf, with its foul reek of molasses; then, a year or so later, the move to Middle Street and more stringent curfews – no leaving his residence for more than four hours at a time, sleeping only at his own residence, needing approval to go beyond Kingstown, and having to state precisely where he was going.

These measures had come after the authorities received word from a ship's captain that Jaja had offered to pay him well to take him to the United States.

The public events that Llewelyn arranged for him during his first year in St. Vincent were still sour in his mouth. He'd played along for a while, biding his time, knowing that they displayed him in public only to play down the true nature of his confinement. He'd played the laughing black man as he recounted stories of the Ashanti War in which he'd aided the British and the wars with his old archenemy, Oko Jumbo. The island's small white elite were amused by his "charmingly picturesque" Creole speech. He'd worn that mask while looking for any opportunity to interact with local Blacks, thinking that one of his own race might help him to escape. One neighbour on Egmont Street became a good friend after he apprehended a man who'd stolen one of Jaja's gold chains and tried to sell it to another neighbour. It was this man, Seymour, who'd told Jaja about a vessel that made a regular stop at St. Vincent on round trips from the U.S.A.

After the discovery, the invitations to cricket matches, concerts by the police band, visits to Government offices, shopping in the leading city stores and private dinner parties at Government House all ceased. The British had thrown their own masks to the floor: Jaja was no guest but a political prisoner who posed a threat to sovereign England. But even if the invitations had been renewed, he'd have pulled back like a sea anemone from the temptation of their bribes. Towards the authorities he cast only sullen looks. He embraced hatred and this venom kept him alive; for over a year it kept him keen and quick.

His home became alive with people who looked like him, who understood his condition and respected his kingship. Their company lifted his spirits. For the first two years of his exile, the local black people had been unaware of the real nature of his presence on the island. The newspapers, owned by members of the merchant class, supported the lie of the king's voluntary presence. The truth was that on orders from the Secretary of State, Johnson, the vice-consul in Nigeria, had trapped Jaja on a British vessel under pretext of holding a meeting to settle a palm-oil trade dispute. Once aboard the vessel, Jaja had been brought to trial in Accra, a town that had no jurisdiction over him as a sovereign king, where he was convicted of breaking a treaty that outlawed other European nations from trading in the Delta hinterlands. The sentence? A hefty fine and five years exile. Britain had rejected his appeals and refused his request to present his case directly to the British Parliament.

★

Now, in the carriage, as he absorbed the green shade flanking the roadsides, Jaja felt a small quickening inside him, like that which chewing a kola nut brought. He inhaled the slow breezes and became aware of how much less he was coughing. Perhaps this hint of alacrity, this apparent improvement in his health, was merely the result of coming to a new place. Whatever the cause, it didn't matter.

As the carriage crawled up Two Mile Hill, one of the guards asked him if, in a few days, he would feel able to accept an invitation from the Governor. Jaja said he would. The guard told him that George Washington's half-brother, Lawrence, had been sent to Barbados nearly a century-and-a-half earlier as a treatment for consumption and that the climate had healing properties, particularly beneficial for diseases of the chest. Jaja suspected the guard was exaggerating, but he had to admit that the air seemed good and that he was already feeling some relief.

The property at Two Mile Hill more than met his needs. In fact, Walmer Cottage far exceeded them. He didn't need a house with so many bedrooms, public rooms, and servants' rooms. Yes, he was a king, but his current circumstances and his nature led him to value frugality. He had not become a king through lavishness, but through his sharp wits and restraint. Taking only well-judged risks, he had risen from being a slave to becoming an eminent tradesman with the Anna Pepple household at Bonny. Slavery's only denial was kingship in the city-state where he had once been a slave. This was why he left Bonny and set up his own kingdom in Opobo, near the banks of the Imo River.

He felt sure Walmer Cottage had been chosen by the British just to extort six pounds five shillings in monthly rent from him, nearly double what he'd paid in St. Vincent. His allowance of eight hundred pounds, permitted by the British and provided by his chiefs in Opobo, would be sent directly to the Barbados Governor who would withhold his rent and miscellaneous expenses that included the care of the his pet dog, Oko Jumbo, maintenance of his carriage, two horses, and a cow. As he got out of the carriage and walked across the pebbled yard, Jaja took in the sheds that lined the back of the two-acre lot. The coach house stood at the far left so that one drove directly out of it along the curving driveway to the Two Mile Hill Road.

He would have needed accommodation like this if any of his wives, sons and servants had been with him, but he was alone. Four months earlier, in St. Vincent, his youngest wife, Patience, had refused to accompany him to Barbados, threatening suicide if she was forced to go. His son, Sunday, had left for study in England. In St. Vincent, servants and relatives had occasionally come from Africa to visit him. Now, as he recalled the modesty of his residence there, his mistrust of the authorities' motives in lodging him at Walmer Cottage heightened. This mistrust increased further when, next morning, the officer who had accompanied him told him to expect another payment to be withheld from his allowance. First Secretary, who would deal with his affairs on behalf of the Governor, would inform him about this.

CHAPTER TWO

Becka heard a knock on the door of their two-room chattel house, and she looked up from the pot she was stirring. Her sister, Frances, was sweeping a corner of the room's dirt-floor. Through the doorway to the bedroom, she could see her ailing mother lying flat on her back. She and Frances had been looking after her since their father died three years ago and their older brother, Fred, had left for Panama to fend for himself. Their chattel stood two miles south of the plantation from which their surname, Jordan, had come. Becka's father had been born there a year before slavery ended. Her grandfather had died on the plantation and had taught his son coopering, the trade he'd lived from all his working life. Mr. Jordan had managed to save enough money to move into the tenantry, though he'd remained bound to the plantation for work and the estate still owned the land on which their chattel stood. Becka had been born in 1872 when her father was thirty-nine years old, and as the youngest she'd been his favourite.

'Mornin'.' A young woman in a maid's uniform and bonnet stood on the makeshift coral-stone steps.

'Patsy, how you? How de baby – my little man?' Patsy lived in the same tenantry and had also worked at Jordan's.

'I awright, Becka. An de baby awright too. Eight months and growing good. How you mudda?'

'Nuh worse. But tings rough, yuh know. Not much wo'k dese days.'

Patsy took a white cloth from between her breasts and opened it to show two phials. She held up the larger of the two and said, 'Gi' dis to she two times a day after she eat. It gwine clean she blood good-good.'

Becka took the gift and said, 'You come all de way down hey to gimme this? I woulda see you at church Sunday… An wuh in de other phial?'

Patsy said nothing and looked away into the distance, her eyes following two blackbirds darting like daggers across the sky.

'Patsy, wha' wrong? Wha' wrong?' Becka asked.

'I gwine just miss you bad.'

'Wuh you mean? Girl, stop talkin' in riddles, nuh.'

'Mr. Brathwaite send me fuh you.'

'Wuh you mean?'

'He say he want you to wo'k fuh he. He waiting.'

Bidding her mother and sister goodbye, Becka took her purse off the hook near the door and she and Patsy stepped outside to enter the carriage parked a few yards down the track in the shade of the mahogany tree. She journeyed in silent apprehension through seas of sugar cane along the khus-khus bordered dirt road that led to Jordan's Plantation.

After her father died from a sudden stroke, life had become even harder for them. Fred had been working on the canal in Panama for two years now; from time to time he sent them money. It was appreciated, but never enough, with Mrs. Jordan needing so much care. As the horses trod on in even rhythm, Becka began to wonder what was in store for her. She knew of young women who'd been summoned by their former masters and returned home spoilt, sometimes carrying the white man's child. She'd wondered if Patsy was one of those women, but could never bring herself to ask. If Patsy ever told her any such thing, she, Becka, would be there to offer comfort. Letting her mind wander, her hand involuntarily clutched the purse.

She had asked, 'Wuh in the other phial you gi' me?'

Patsy leaned over and whispered, 'Pure oleander juice. It ain' mix wid nuthing,'

The quiet of Sundays always struck Becka. The villagers were mostly at home. Washed clothes were spread out to dry on coral stones at the sides of the houses. Pots were on fires. The men, after sleeping late, would be fixing things around the house: a broken chair leg, a broken chicken coop door. Children were running about in the yards making sport, playing fowlcock with the beaked

12

quarters of mahogany pods or pitching marbles. It was not a quietness created by inactivity, but by the attitude that Sunday called for: some control, some respect for the Lord's day, so one could speak freely, but not too loudly, could hammer a nail for oneself, but not too noisily.

Taking in the scene, Becka drank in the morning sun, felt the March breezes roll over her face, and responded with a long, wide-armed stretch. The driver slowed the carriage to a halt and Becka watched Patsy wedge her bundle under her arm, raise her cotton skirt and step onto the track hardened over the years by thousands of walking and running feet. She saw her friend walk over to the driver, and signal him to wait. Becka stepped out of the carriage, and the two of them walked out of earshot of the driver to talk.

Becka listened as Patsy urged her not to hesitate to use the oleander if ever she feared being taken advantage of. Talk was that the new owner of Jordan's, Cheeseman Moe Brathwaite, always got the maid (whom Becka might be replacing) to bring him a cup of tea after he'd had his way with one of the female workers.

'Dah would be de time to sneak it in,' Patsy said. 'If it doan kill he, it goin' mess-up he brain or mek he balls dry-up.'

Becka reflected that maybe Patsy was as safe as any young woman could hope to be, working on an estate.

As soon as Becka was back in the carriage, the driver tipped back his old felt hat, flicked the reins, and the two horses started moving again. She looked back to see Patsy by her doorway waving a hand.

Fields of partially-harvested canes surrounded the last mile of their journey. As the carriage neared its destination, Becka could not stop thinking about the risks ahead. But she needed work if her family was to survive. She was not naïve. Women friends in the tenantry had told her things. As a house servant, you had to live there, not in your own chattel two or three miles away. You had to be ready to respond instantly to the needs of the family you served. You might have to pick some aloes from the yard to apply to one of the children's bruises, or make a late-night beverage for the master or lady of the house, or, deeper in the night, when most everyone slept and the only sounds were the whistling frogs and crickets, you might have to hoist your nightdress when your door opened and the master's heavy-set body filled the doorway, a smile on his beet-red face.

As Jordan's came into view, Becka breathed deeply, her fears flitting like bats in her head. Should she ask the driver to take her back? He probably wouldn't or couldn't. She could hop off the carriage and run back home. She was strong and quick with good sturdy legs. But her sick mother waited there. Her sister, too, was also unemployed. She made a dress or skirt for somebody here and there, sometimes going to a jig with one of the villagers and allowing him to touch and know her in an unspoken negotiation through which she'd secure a few pence or some ground provisions.

The carriage pulled into the plantation yard. Blackbirds squawked in the high branches of the mahogany trees. This job would give her the security she and her family needed. She squeezed the purse she was carrying, feeling where the phial nested.

CHAPTER THREE

Jaja rose on the fingers of dawn. He still moved slowly and still coughed, but he felt brighter since his arrival. With a wide, slow-motion gesture (as if he were summoning his people to hear some important proclamation), he hoisted one of the eastern sash windows and unlatched and pushed open the green wooden louvres behind it. He held out his arms, closed his eyes and inhaled the morning air. The air here, though warmer, was less humid than in St. Vincent. It carried no chills and came in a constant flow, like wine with a pleasant aftertaste, or like the peaceful silence following a sparrow's trill. In St. Vincent, the rough sea breezes that swept through his room in Kingstown, coupled with the depressions of forced exile, had been too much for him. Colonial Surgeon Newsam, after thoroughly examining Jaja, had told him, 'The late high winds and heavy rains mixed with this infernally hot weather haven't helped your health, Jaja. I can see that you've lost appetite and have not been sleeping well. If anything can be done for you, even now, it could be too late.'

'I wish to spend my remaining days in Opobo, to die among my people,' Jaja replied, looking towards Administrator Llewelyn who had entered the room.

'I will make my recommendations,' he said, 'but you will have to give us your written pledge that if you were repatriated, you would refrain from any political activity in the Delta region. That's my one condition. Would you agree to that?'

Jaja nodded.

Outside the room, Newsam said, 'I know that the king has had a coffin ordered. He's deeply depressed and grieving over his exile. He's been coughing incessantly and complaining of chest

15

pains. He has pneumonia and bronchitis – the last, I'm afraid, being of the chronic kind.'

'He's not a young man. How old is he? Sixty? Seventy?' Llewelyn said. 'It would not look good if he died on us.'

'It's imperative then that he be moved to a drier, more salubrious climate. I'd recommend Barbados. What do you think?'

'He would be better off there,' Llewelyn agreed. 'When he's recovered enough for travel, we'll arrange to have him transferred. We must hasten to get all the paperwork in place.'

Before leaving St. Vincent, Jaja had been so depressed he wrote his will, naming Patience as executrix.

Now, through the second-storey bedroom window, Jaja saw the distant St. George valley undulating in an expanse of soft deep greens, its borders sharpened by the sunlight. From there, his eyes arced to the east and the west. Hillsides dotted with white houses. Coconut palms and trees waving in welcome and farewell.

Jaja thought he heard a knock on the house door. It came again. It couldn't be one of the guards whose raps were always loud and irritating. Jaja put on his robe and looked down from the window.

'Mornin',' a young woman called up. She wore a white bonnet and a white, long-sleeved cotton dress that reached to mid-calf. 'I name Becka. Mister Brathwaite send me. I is you servant and nurse.'

'Good morning. The constable will let you in, me girl,' Jaja said.

The constable soon appeared and let the young woman in.

A little later, Becka knocked and came in with fresh bed-linen, and briskly began to change the sheets and pillow cases. She looked about eighteen years of age, close to that of his youngest wife, Patience, whom he still missed exceedingly. Like Patience, this girl was well-built and full-breasted. She had, he sensed, an agreeable disposition. His heart bucked in gladness as he watched her confident coltish steps whisk across the room with the bundle of old linen, keenly aware of Jaja's eyes on her.

She paused by the door and said, 'Mister Jaja, leh me know if you need anything. Mr. Brathwaite say you on special food and he gimme a list o' things to cook fo' you. You gwine be alright. I going now and fix you breakfast.'

'All right, me girl,' Jaja said. 'I coming down shortly to you.'

When Jaja took his bath he noted that his skin wasn't as clammy and as sweaty as before. Then he put on cotton pants, a colourful shirt, and sandals. He felt a little tingling in his throat and coughed into a handkerchief. He was relieved to find that, this time, there was no greenish-yellow sputum, no blood. He did, though, still feel weary and his joints and muscles ached. As he made his way unsteadily down the staircase, he began to doubt whether he would make it by himself. On the day he'd arrived, the two guards had helped him up to his room. He was about to call for one of them when Becka appeared near the foot of the staircase, carrying breakfast on a tray. She saw him grasping the railing.

'You awright, Mr. Jaja? You awright?' She placed the tray on a side table and hurried up to him. She placed her right arm under his shoulder and slowly guided him down the remaining steps.

'Yes... yes... yes. Thank you, me girl,' Jaja said. Becka steered him to the dining room and sat him down. Then she retrieved the breakfast tray and placed the food before him: a glass of lemon juice, a bowl of oatmeal, and fresh, warm cow's milk.

'I goin' come back when you done,' she said.

Jaja nodded and said, 'Call de guard here.'

The constable arrived shortly afterwards, and Jaja told him that, for now, he'd prefer to sleep in a guest room on the ground floor so as not to aggravate his sore muscles and joints by going up and down the staircase.

'You can leave my upstairs bedroom as it be,' Jaja said, 'for I expect sleep back in it before too long.'

'I'll have it arranged,' the constable said and returned to his second-floor station at the back of the house.

When Becka returned, Jaja informed her of the arrangement and asked her to bring his clothes and medicines down to where he'd be sleeping. Jaja saw Becka look at his empty plate. She'd clearly been informed of his condition – the inflammation of his lungs and the resulting loss of appetite. He, too, looked at the empty plate. Perhaps he might get better and his regular weight return. They looked at each other and smiled.

CHAPTER FOUR

Becka opened the pantry door to see what she could prepare for the king's lunch and dinner. The shelves brimmed with ground provisions grown at Jordans – sweet potatoes, yams, eddoes and pumpkins. Worrell, Walmer Cottage's gardener and handyman, would bring her lettuce from the garden he tended a couple of hundred feet from the north end of the house, but hidden from it by guava, sapodilla, mango, sour-sop trees, and coconut palms. Here, he grew okra, cabbage, spinach, beets, and herbs such as thyme, marjoram, sage, basil, mint and chives.

'Becka! Becka! Look hey!' It was Worrell calling from the yard. She hated being disturbed when she was in the middle of her chores – she was cooking the king a vegetable soup for lunch – but went out to the yard to see what Worrell wanted. He was standing next to a large container about six feet tall. She heard the sound of horses's hooves and saw the back of a large cart moving like a beetle along the path that led to Two Mile Hill Road.

'Dese goods just get hey from Trafalgar House. I gwine tek dem out-o-de big box hey and you can tek dem in,' Worrell said. Becka sighed, exerting her authority as the controller of all things pertaining to the house. Only she and the king really lived here. The guards, the one stationed outside the side door and the other at the top of the back outer staircase, worked in rotation with other guards. Worrell lived in a nearby tenantry. She knew Worrell liked her, but she had no romantic inclinations towards him whatsoever. She was just happy that she wasn't working at the plantation. No sooner had Mr. Brathwaite, thumbs in his watch-dangling waistcoat, offered her the job at the cottage just outside Bridgetown, than Patsy's words sprang to her head: *I gwine miss you bad*. Patsy had obviously known where Mr. Brathwaite intended to send her, though she had also thought it wise to prepare Becka for the worst with her wisdom laced with oleander juice. Perhaps Brathwaite had given Patsy this information in the hope that it would make her feel comfortable with his offer. And though she wasn't so naïve as to think that Walmer Cottage provided complete immunity from Mr. Brathwaite – if he got any ideas – the fact that he rarely stayed at this residence, and its distance from Jordans, made her feel more at ease.

Worrell said, 'I ask de driver if dese things fo' de king and he say, "De king? Who king dah? Wha' king you talking 'bout?" He did real surprise. I ask he if he didn' hear 'bout de African king that Queen Victoria send down hey as a pris'na?'

Becka said, 'Even up in de country people hear 'bout um. Some country vendors was down there when he come in at de Wharf. One o' dem tell my sister.'

Adjusting his brown felt hat, Worrell said, 'Well, de driver sey he hear 'bout he, but didn' know de goods he bring up was for he. Dah is wha' surprise he. Before he pull out – jus' befo' you come down – he stare at me and sey, "Wha' king wha'? He could be a king? Wha' sorta king could let dem English people capture he and send he down hey so?"'

Becka felt a defensive wind billow inside her.

'Dat driver is a idiot, a stupid idiot. Doan pay him nuh mind.' Her intensity brought Worrell back to his task. He fumbled a pocket knife from his worn gaberdines and began to break the seals on the carton. Becka saw the words **TRAFALGAR HOUSE** stamped in bold block capitals and, in smaller capitals, RECEIVED FROM LONDON, LIVERPOOL, AND NEW YORK. Worrell removed cases of Swiss-manufactured condensed milk, Neave's oatmeal, Robinson's patent barley, and Fry's cocoa and chocolate sticks. As he carried the items to the door, Worrell, muscular and short, moved back and forth like a rubber ball, allowing Becka to imagine she heard tuk-band music accompanying him. Bags of sago and tapioca, pears and apples, bags of rice, currants, citron peel and pudding raisins, white and pink sugared almonds, conversation and peppermint lozenges, lemon drops, white and pink corianders, nonpareil comfits, acidulated pear drops, twisted barley sugar, clanging balls, and a bottle or two of whiskey made their way into the house. Some of these items would not be good for the king, and Becka was determined to protect him. Only occasional sweets for him. And certainly none of the scotch, some of which she'd already discovered in a cabinet. Her duty was to nurse him back to full health.

After Worrell had unloaded all the items and the guard had inspected them, Becka took most of the lighter goods inside to stack in the pantry. When she came outside again, Worrell had flattened the carton by cutting it apart with his knife. He helped her take the remaining cases inside. As he turned to go, Becka said, 'Worrell, see if you can get some fish fo' me, some good albacore or cavali or dolphin fish. I want it fo' dinner, hear?' He turned, smiled at her, and winked. Becka playfully shooed him away with a sweep of the back of her hand.

Around lunchtime, one of the guards came inside with a letter for Jaja. He was sitting in one of the public rooms reading the *Barbados Globe,* which carried a small news story about him. It said nothing about his status as an exile and political prisoner, only about his arrival on Sunday at the Wharf and the rowdiness of the crowd who surrounded the carriage. It also spoke about a law passed by the Assembly before his arrival which 'regulated and defined the position of certain persons while in Barbados'.

Jaja opened the Governor's letter and soon started shaking his head. There would now be two further deductions from his allowance – for the maid and nursing services to the amount of two pounds three shillings monthly, and a monthly rental of two pounds for the carriage. The passing of the regulatory law by the local Assembly related directly to him. The officials were evidently determined not to allow the colony to be put to any expense because of his stay on the island. The Governor also wrote that in the morning Jaja was to receive his assistant who would come to take him into the city. 'If you're able,' the letter read, 'it would be advantageous to your constitution to be up and about as much as you can. The fresh air, light activity and the scenery will benefit your health greatly.'

The king felt strengthened by Becka's soup. After the meal, he took a light cotton shawl and, wrapping it around his shoulders, stepped out into the yard and whistled three bird notes. He imagined Oko Jumbo uncoiling from his mat in the kennel in the back corner of the yard. His black bull terrier emerged and came towards him, tongue lolling, his short pig-like tail wagging. Jaja lowered himself and rubbed the crown of the dog's head. Laughing, he said, 'Oko, I is you master now. You slaughtered my men at Bonny with thirty-two-pounds carronades, you scattered their skulls in every direction. But the Andoni's Iyobulo favoured me and let me set-up my kingdom next to them. I paralysed you by closing my markets to you for a thousand years. I live as you master now.' Jaja's shoulders shook with merriment as he recalled his old nemesis.

He and Oko passed the south-eastern side of the house. The green fan of a large sisal plant bristled into the air in the corner and a low hedge of purple hibiscus led them along the eastern fringe of the property where a gate led out to Two Mile Hill Road. Jaja and Oko went in the opposite direction along the side of the house ringed with crotons and taller ornamentals frothing with white hibiscus-like flowers. They soon reached the gardens at the northern tip of the house where the St. George valley could be seen in the distance. Ornamental coral-stone pots decorated with images of dancing nymphs, angels, and cupidons overflowed with flowering plants. Passing these, he saw a large tree which he immediately recognized. It was the sacred baobab. Jaja approached it reverently, then his steps quickened, as though he'd found some lost treasure. He stood at the base of the tree, took a small bottle from his pocket, uncapped it, and sprinkled the rum which he'd discovered in a cabinet next to several bottles of scotch, on to the base of the trunk. His lips moved in prayer.

He sat down on a coral-stone bench and inhaled the fresh air. He looked into the deep cerulean sky in which pure-white puffy clouds were moving, just perceptibly. He stayed there until he suddenly, happily, realized he'd left his cane back in his room. He hadn't needed it. He and Oko rose and headed back to the house which, from this perspective, showed a truer picture of its size. It certainly wasn't the size of a plantation house, but it was no tiny cottage either. Jaja put Oko in his kennel and, passing the impassive guard, went to his room to rest until dinner.

CHAPTER FIVE

Around three-thirty, Becka heard a knock on the door and opened it to find Worrell standing there with a bunch of fish strung together on a line. He looked pleased with himself. Although he hadn't caught them himself, he had a look of accomplishment that Becka interpreted as having to do with how he felt about her. This interpretation was confirmed when, getting no response, Worrell said, 'How you feel 'bout de king in dey and you in dey, in de same house, just two o' unna?'

'You see dem guards dey? One at de side and the udder one at de back? You tink I won' scream down de place, if Mr. Jaja try something and won' leh me 'lone?'

'Is enough fo' people start talkin' talk.'

'Leh dum talk, nuh. Now, on de udder hand, if I tek a likin' to he, maybe he might mek me he queen.' Becka twisted her body and crossed her feet in a squirming tease designed to irritate Worrell.

'Wuh you talkin' 'bout, Becka, You cyan see he got one foot in de grave? Wuh you would want wid he? Wuh he can do fo' you?'

'He's a king.'

'And wuh 'bout me, Becka? I been looking at you evuh since you come hey. I like yuh, Becka.'

'I like you too, Worrell,' she said. 'but not de same way you like me. De cavalis look fresh and good. Wuh part you get dum from?' Becka extended her hands to take the catch.

'Down by Cheapside, as usual. An' I bring something extra fuh you, Becka.' Worrell reached into the large side pocket of his jacket and withdrew something wrapped in newspaper. He parted it to reveal a one-pound cut of dolphin fish.

'Just fo' you, Becka,' Worrell said. 'I got it just fo' you.'

'T'anks, Worrell. T'ank yuh, hear?'

'Awright. I 'gine down hey.'

After putting the meat in a container in the kitchen, Becka approached the king's door and carefully opened it. He appeared sound asleep. As she stood watching him, she knew that while she'd deliberately teased Worrell by suggesting she liked the king, her growing good feeling towards Jaja was real. Yes, she felt sorry for him as he told her bits and pieces of the circumstances that had brought him to Barbados. 'Those British want to kill me,' he'd told her. 'They fine me plenty money at mock trial, took me hard-earned money, and too besides, exile me from me native land for five years. I now start the fourth year of my exile, an old man with all the ailments you now see me have.' It had surprised her when she'd so vigorously defended him from the carriage driver's impertinent remarks earlier in the day. She was coming to realize that she cared for Jaja more than she'd ever intended.

It seemed to her that Jaja's broad face revealed a capacity for both empathy and judgment. It contained softness but also a hardness, a power that sprang from his broad shoulders and erect posture. The fact that he was slightly knockkneed didn't bother her. He was not a young man and she knew of his ailments. But there was something that charmed her about him that she felt had to do with the way he carried himself, the confident way he looked at her as if he knew everything she was thinking and feeling; something calming, too, some quality of warmth and gentleness conveyed through his gaze. When his soft and steady eyes looked at her, she felt she was the only person in the world, the only one Jaja cared about. He was a rock buffeted by the sea, unflinching, unmoving, even though over time it would suffer inevitable erosion. She felt her spirit leaning towards him.

Jaja was not quite asleep, but his mind was elsewhere… *Will Banigo… Warribo… Oko Jumbo barking in Manilla canoe-houses. Like me they been slaves… I from the age of twelve. When I mek man, my Anna Pepple sponsor me in trade cause they know I could be trusted. They know me got drive and they underwrite me and I get funds from me own trading and from de supercargoe "dashes" I save. I loyal… I clever… I fearless. When a trader offer me gin, I say, 'Drink mek man fool.' So my level-head get me fame throughout Delta, and I buy me first canoe, recruit me own boatmen, start transporting puncheons to traders on coast… My sunrise grow bright and brighter…*

Oko was shining too, securing support from missionaries, sending he son John to study in England, himself learning to read and write. Nothing wrong with that, but when he say him a Christian, declare iguana no more Bonny juju, abolish practice to kill twins at birth, that is when I say no more of his foolishness, his treachery… So I recoil from the white man markings I see on Oko forehead, from the small beady eyes sunk deep as a well, and set close together and high up on his black piercing face, glinting wit' cunning… full o' deceit. I recoil from his white man desire, and I trust me old friend no more. One thing to learn what you can from white man to add to our prosperity… quite another to receive his white markings, abandon our ways, the ways of the ancients…

…Banigo's house catch-a-fire in Lagos with ailing Chief Annie Stewart. Commotion like monkeys hunted in mangrove branches. Me and me men run to put the fire out. A strong wind hoists a burning cinder which lodges in a hut in my section of the town. Two-thirds of that place perish in flames. My sister scorched to death. Oh I grieve… But oh I rebuild in Mimina Village near the big Imo markets. Oko get so vex, the surface of his face look like it contain craters boiling with sulphur… His flat forehead, long face come alive with readiness for war… I see the distance from the tip of Oko's nose to his eyes is much greater than from his eyes to the top of his skull. I wish to possess that blood-dripping skull in battle after removing the small stiff ears with my bush knife and severing his head from his long neck. Anna Pepple House woman draw water from Manilla House pond. Oko calls for war, but I, Jaja, I keep back for a time. Too besides, I still have debts owed to supercargoes. So when Oko press for war, I bury me treasures in surrounding villages, plant cannons, dig deep trenches… until I hear a Manilla shot… the first gun-shot of war…

'How you feelin'?' Becka asked.

'Very good, me girl,' he said, about to sip the fish soup. 'My strength like it coming back since I come here. In two days I feeling strong again.' Becka had left her apron in the kitchen and sat next to the king with her own serving of soup. She raised the spoon to her mouth. Steam coiled from their bowls.

'You sleeping strong. Dah is good. And you appetite a lot better. I put mushrooms, curbs, cabbage, carrots, and sweet potatoes in you fish soup, along wid dill and basil fuh flavuh.'

'I swear it is you hand mekking me strong.' Jaja was looking steadily at her. She had the physical traits of all his wives, well-built, at once soft and muscular.

'Mind de fly don' get in you soup,' Becka said, aware of his interest and enjoying it.

After Becka had finished cleaning the cooking utensils and putting them away, Jaja called her into the meeting room where he was reading and said, 'You remind me about somebody I know.'

'And who dah is?'

'My wife, Patience. Who was my wife. She lef' me. She won' leave St. Vincent and come with me.'

'I sorry, Jaja. You say she *was* you wife?'

'She come from her place called Long Elve. She is not a native of my place, Opobo.'

'I feel sorry fo' you.'

'I beg the Administrator. I say, "She should be here with me cause when I go back to my country, I must have a-plenty trouble if she not with me. When I reach my place, her father will ask me where is his daughter. When I tell him she won't come, he will say why I come and not bring her. It must bring trouble upon me."'

'So wuh he say?'

'He say he would look into the matter. I tell him, "She says she has no family and that is not true. All of them is living. She say if she must go, she will drown herself and that she cannot do." I say to him, "Tell the governor to send her to me. If you do that for me you serve me. I beg your god and my god to put it in her heart to come. She talks of drowning herself and that she cannot do."'

'And wuh de governor do?'

'What they always do. Nothing. Tomorrow I see governor here and ask if there is anything he can do. But...' Jaja's voice had lowered considerably, 'I don't really wish no more.'

Perhaps it was the way he'd looked at her over the past day or so, perhaps the shared pleasure of the fish soup, the sympathy she felt for his fate at the hands of the English, or now his story of rejection by the woman who was to be his wife that aroused Becka's desire to take the king in her arms and comfort him. And that maternal desire, she discovered to her surprise, soon began to give way to another form of desire she felt moving up her thighs.

She nodded toward her room. The sun was on the rim of the horizon so Becka went to light the candles in the hall way. When she reached her room, Jaja was standing by the door. Inside, she lit the three candles on a chest of drawers. Glancing through the open window, she saw the fingers of the crimson sunset high up in the sky. She closed the window, let her garments fall, and lay on the small cot. As Jaja removed his shirt, she saw the cowry-shell necklace, the shells smooth and gleaming, against his black skin.

CHAPTER SIX

Jaja was already dressed in suit and bow-tie when Becka came to tell him the First Secretary had arrived.

'I want you go back with me to Opobo, please God,' he said to Becka, 'when my time here end two years from now – though it be my burning wish to leave before then.'

Becka looked at him without expression, as though she was studying him, as though she did not believe him.

'You would like it in my place,' he continued. 'Opobo cocks crow with the rising sun and with same strength they do here. We call our town the Home of Peace. Mek we go?' Jaja smiled as Becka slid forward to fix his slanting collar. Then, twisting her body in her teasing way, she lightly patted his shoulder.

She said, 'I got tuh stay hey tuh help tek care o' my mudda. I cyan "mek me go".' They both laughed.

'I understand, me girl,' Jaja said, 'but, please God, one day you might. Where your mother's place?'

'In de country. I goin' tuh see she on de weekend.'

'How you get there?' Jaja asked.

'Walk. I got good strong legs.'

Jaja gazed at them with an affirmative smile. 'I will take you in my carriage. You will guide, and I drive… if that be well with you.'

Becka told him they could go on Sunday, and it was then that Jaja decided that after his afternoon nap, he'd take the carriage for a short ride along Two Mile Hill, to practice.

★

The Assistant First Secretary, dressed in tweed suit and waistcoat, rose hesitantly from his caned mahogany chair when Jaja appeared in the doorway of the sitting room, as if he wasn't sure of the protocol. A king, but a black man who was a prisoner of Her Majesty's government. As Jaja walked toward him, he started to proffer a hand, but then withdrew it.

Jaja pretended not to notice and said, 'Good morning. I am Jaja. You British give me that name 'cause you could not pronounce my true name, Jubo Jubogha.'

'Good morning,' the Assistant First Secretary said, and sensing a gateway of levity through which he might redeem his discomfort, he added, 'How should I address you, then? Jaja or Jumo... Jujo Ju...?'

'Jaja.' The king laughed in a restrained way.

The First Secretary laughed too, and wondered if this was a man you could warm to.

He took a fob watch from his pocket, glanced at it and said, 'The Governor's waiting to greet you. Shall we go?'

The driver was ready to leave. A light breeze played with the leaves of mahoganies, pink cassias, and crotons as Jaja and the First Secretary got into the carriage. The driver dourly flicked the reins and the horse began its slow clippity-clops along the pebbled driveway. The chirpings of sparrows accompanied the moving vehicle, their choruses occasionally punctuated by the plaintive cry of a wood dove.

They passed men and women in field clothing, cutlasses in their hands, heading north, most likely to St. George and Jordan's Plantation, some perhaps even further, to St. Andrew or St. John. The carriage moved up Government Hill and pulled into the driveway of the governor's residence. Jaja was trying hard to fight the gloom that came over him in anticipation of what he knew would be British treachery. But he was a fighter, a warrior. His palace contained coats and shawls matted with the hair and the blood of his enemies, gourds garlanded with the jawbones and teeth of his foes. He had drunk palm wine from a gourd fixed to the top of an enemy's skull. At a festival when the spirit of Opobo danced in masquerade on the galvanized roof of his palace, he'd raised that skull to his mouth, scornful in his pledge to deny the British victory, though the odds against him were heavy. Even if defeated, he would never give them the satisfaction of seeing him fall to the floor and beg.

Governor Sendall said, 'Welcome, Jaja. How are you? We'll have lunch on the back porch as the breezes today are most light and agreeable.' Jaja groaned inwardly as the Governor ushered him and the First Secretary into the foyer of the living room. The Governor spoke with the same feigned politeness Jaja had encountered in St. Vincent. He knew that before too long the mask of these false sentiments would fall to reveal their true feelings.

'I feeling much better since my arrival,' Jaja said. 'Though I fear something happen to my people whilst I am away from them. I am hoping you might convince your Queen to issue pardon on my behalf. I have been in this exile some three years now.'

'I'm afraid, Jaja, that only an emergency might allow such a request. The British Crown…' he turned to look at the portrait of Queen Victoria hanging in its elaborate gilded frame, 'cannot suspend it's judgments. But, let's talk about pleasanter subjects, shall we? How are you settling in over at Two Mile Hill?'

'Will you send a dispatch to the Queen? Could that be done?'

'We'll look into that,' Sendall said.

Jaja didn't want to waste time on superficial courtesies. Yet, he knew he had to be careful not to alienate or anger the Governor, who might have some influence in alleviating his circumstances. As they walked through the house, Jaja noted the branched candelabras hanging from the gold-panelled ceiling, the antique mantels and huge paintings on the walls. He reflected that this house and his palace shared a common sense of power that differed only in style and execution. His wooden house had two storeys and its front entrance was hooded by a white porch supported on Doric pillars. As here there was a brass knocker on the front door for visitors to announce their arrival, and wooden louvred shutters to keep out the heat and glare and protect the glass sash windows during storms. The only difference of these houses lay in the materials. The Governor's was made of coral stone whereas his was made of wood.

He and the First Secretary took their seats at the circular table where Mrs. Sendall, dainty in pink chiffon, already sat with another woman. They rose to be introduced. Her companion was her sister who was visiting from England. A sleeping black Labrador curled on a mat in a corner of the porch.

The porch looked out onto an enormous yard with a large mahogany tree in the centre, its base circled with red bricks and ferns, with a wooden bench in the shade of its canopy. Ripe coconuts dangled like full udders from the several palms that ringed the yard. Banana trees glistened in the sun; royal palm fronds swayed; a pink cassia thrust out its long spikes of bloom; two flamboyants raged in red; and pink and white frangipanis glowed with their round-petalled stars. Trees like these also grew in Opobo, and this recognition quickened the king.

Mrs. Sendall's sister wanted to know how Jaja's kingdom was surviving since his exile.

He said, 'My chiefs are keeping the town well. They're keeping Opobo as well as they can, and that be true.'

The Governor sat with a wry look on his face, a look, Jaja knew, that conveyed his knowledge of what was probably happening in Opobo, where the British were no doubt continuing their aggressive initiatives into the hinterland, muscling in on the trade in palm oil, and establishing trading posts, mission schools and – to protect that presence – establishing colonial government. They would extract the oil themselves, fling his traders aside like flies and ship the produce in their own puncheons down the wide Imo River to the coast where it would be exported to England for their oil lamps and to make candles and soaps.

Emma! What had become of her and the elementary school she'd established that, unlike the mission schools, reinforced his country's customs and religious practices? Jaja had been so impressed by her from the day she'd arrived from Liberia. She was one of the Black Americans who'd returned to Africa from the United States. Emma White. One of Jaja's Liberian friends, Sao Benson, had recommended her during a visit when they had discussed education in Opobo and the need for more traditional teachers to counter the influence of the mission schools. Jaja had given Emma his name and her own hut to protect her, but she was not one of his wives. With his name she would be safe. He'd been impressed by her force of character and her talents. With her high skills in reading and writing and her perfectly-spoken English, she'd become his secretary and advisor, reading over the correspondence sent to him by the British consuls during the trade dispute. She'd been at his side each day in the Accra courtroom when he was tried and sentenced.

Unhappiness began to nudge Jaja, so he decided to broach a new subject.

'The silver-mounted sword of honour from your queen still in my compound,' he said. 'And that be true.'

'Really?' Mrs. Sendall said. 'And how did that happen, pray?'

Her husband said, 'Jaja is referring to the Ashanti War, my dear. One of our victories, I must add. I believe he will tell us the story.'

'The sword carries inscription: "Presented by command of her Majesty the Queen of Great Britain and Ireland as a mark of esteem and friendship to King Jaja of Opobo." It was presented in April 1875 by Consul Harthy in the presence of a Mr. Knight and a Mr. Moore, both mercantile agents from Bonny who travelled to Opobo to witness presentation ceremony.'

'How nice,' Mrs. Sendall said.

'Remarkable,' said her sister.

'But Jaja,' the Governor said, 'do tell the ladies how your country came to be involved in the Ashanti War. They love history and who better to tell them than one who played such a vital role.'

Jaja knew he had to be very careful what he said. He could not risk offending the Queen's representative who was inviting him to trespass on diplomatically fragile territory. Certain topics were best left untouched.

'I remember it well,' Jaja said. 'November, 1873. Your Captain Nicol arrived at my place, Opobo, seeking aid for expedition to punish Ashanti. I provide fifty-three men for payment of one shilling per day and food. They went with Nicol after we sign statement that this be for one time and not precedent.'

Mrs Sendall winced and turned her face away. Her sister's face stiffened. The Governor and his assistant smiled encouragingly.

Jaja continued: 'Why I ally against Ashanti?' His eyes briefly settled on each person seated at the table. When the pause had been long enough, he said, 'To prove to British that black man could rescue his army.'

The women looked at the Governor for some response, but it

seemed as if a cloud of contemplation had settled on him, making speech impossible. When an aproned servant appeared with a pitcher of cold lemonade, her presence allowed the Governor and his family to regain their composure. Glasses and napkins had already been laid on the table. The two women seized glasses of lemonade and began to sip.

'Thank you, Mabel,' Mrs. Sendall sighed.

As Mabel bowed and turned to leave, another servant appeared with five plates of mutton and rice on a large wicker tray. The Governor blessed the meal, and Jaja felt the mutton melt in his mouth. It tasted almost as delicious as the kind he ate in Opobo. Beckoning the servant, he asked her for a second serving, nodding emphatically to underscore his wish and his pleasure. She returned with a spiced, well-done portion of leg, chuckling silently as she retreated into the house.

CHAPTER SEVEN

From the upstairs room that she was dusting and airing, Becka saw the horse and carriage moving along the driveway. As it came up alongside the house and Jaja got out, she could see his face was tightly-drawn. She went down to meet him, but thought it best not to engage him in any conversation. She'd made his favourite fish and vegetable soup which he would eat later in the afternoon. She remembered the same tired old face the day he arrived, the swollen knees, the coughing. She was determined to give him the best care to prevent any relapse.

Around four o'clock, some time after she'd given Jaja his lunch and returned to the pantry to prepare food for the evening meal, she heard a commotion outside. Worrell was exchanging words with Jaja in the yard.

'You cyan tell me wha' tuh do,' Worrell was saying. 'I doan wuk fo' you. I wuk fo' Mr. Brathwaithe.'

'Wuh goin' on here?' Becka demanded from the doorway.

'De king want me wash he ole ugly dog. Mr. Brathwaite doan pay me tuh wash nuhbody dog.' Worrell was livid with anger.

'Do you know I can have you hanged or skinned alive for disobeying me?'

'Disobeying you? Who you...?'

'I am speaking! Do not interrupt! You serve me!' Jaja barked, and Oko Jumbo, standing next to him, barked as well. Becka saw a rope in Jaja's hand. The king was evidently serious in his desire to strangle Worrell, though she doubted he would succeed, being almost twice Worrell's age.

She placed a hand on Jaja's shoulder. The king glared at Worrell. 'Go from before me before I tear to you to pieces with my bare hands!' Worrell held his ground, ready to fire back.

'Worrell, the ice…' Becka said. Worrell, still glaring at Jaja and cursing loudly, went to bring a horse from the stable to attach it to the cart. Becka had asked him to collect a block of ice from the Central Ice House in Roebuck Street, the same business from which Mr. Brathwaite had rented Jaja's carriage. When the cart reached the south-eastern side of the house, Worrell turned his head and called, 'She too young fuh you. She ain' want nuh dry-up old man like you.'

Becka always found the ways of men amusing, their furious need to keep face and to win any contest when a woman was present or love was being sought. It must be hard to be a man. Jaja's show of temper was no doubt to do with his visit to the Governor and Worrell's reactions had more to do with her than Jaja's request. She knew of Jaja's politeness and generosity (the gold chain around her neck) and that Worrell would have been generously compensated for bathing the dog. She was flattered by Worrell's attentions, but – and it surprised her again – her feelings for the king went beyond anything she could have imagined.

When Worrell returned from the city again, now in the carriage, he had a passenger with him. Becka was preparing the evening meal when she heard the crunch of wheels on the cobbled yard outside. When she came to the door, she saw a black buckled boot and striped black pants swinging out from the carriage's side. A hand holding a cane came next, followed by the entire person of Mr. Brathwaite. He looked about him, smiling proprietorially.

'How is everything coming along here, Becka?' he asked as he nodded to the guard and entered the house.

'Ev'rything good, Sir,' Becka replied, taking his coat and hanging it on the hall-tree in the front room. The guards knew who he was. Brathwaite had come before with the First Secretary and the two police constables assigned to guard the king.

'I can get you something, Sir?'

'I will take a Scotch just before dinner, Becka. But nothing right now.'

'Very well, Sir.'

'And how is our famous guest? I have not met him since he arrived. I must meet him at once – the king.'

'I will get him for you, Sir. He ujahly does get a rest before dinner.'

Becka returned with Jaja who had returned to his upstairs room, the swelling of his knees having diminished. The caned mahogany chair creaked as Mr. Brathwaite rose from his seat and apologized to Jaja for the intrusion. He assured him that his visit was in accordance with the agreement he'd made with the governor.

'Every now and then (very rarely), I must stay at Walmer's to conduct business in the city. Otherwise I would have to bear the wear and tear of travelling back and forth between St. George and Bridgetown on a daily basis. Seven hours one way. I'll stay out of your way. Of that you can be sure.'

Becka left the two men talking and went to prepare supper. In Jaja's presence her fears concerning Mr. Brathwaite had declined. When she returned almost an hour later with meals on a tray for them, the two men were still in conversation. Mr. Brathwaite was saying, 'There was an article in *The Globe*. But I think it said "Opobo". You said "Opubo."'

'The British destroy everything of Black man in Africa. Even our names and place names. Opubo name from the founder of our great city, Bonny, who died thirty years before I found my own country. I name my kingdom after him. They did same thing with my name.'

'Your name?'

'Jaja is a corruption of my true name, Jubo Jubogha.'

'The Governor's a sneaky little devil, isn't he?' Brathwaite said. 'Had I known how important your kingdom is, I could have obtained a carriage even more fit for your station, drawn by two horses. I wonder why he didn't tell me. I must bring this to his attention next time I'm afforded the privilege of his company.'

'You say someone tell you about my kingdom.'

'Mr. Whitfield, from whom I rented the carriage for your use (and who provides your ice), well, one of his staff told him my man Worrell was saying you were a king from Africa and loaded with jewels and money. Because of that, I'm sure Whitfield increased the cost of the blocks of ice, and why he's talking of increasing the carriage rent from next week. What a scoundrel that man Whitfield is!'

Becka, still standing by the table said, 'Worrell was just mekking conversation. You know he didn' mean no'thing by it.' But she began to wonder if Worrell's jealousy might not have been the motivation for his revelations, particularly the details about Jaja's wealth.

'We shall see. That's why I'm staying over a night or two, to see if I can bring Whitfield to a more agreeable position. If I can't, Worrell will have to pay for his big mouth. Taking the difference from his pay would be a suitable measure. If he doesn't like that, he can find himself another job.'

'Have mercy, Sir,' Becka said. 'I sure he got plenty chil'run to feed.'

Mr. Brathwaite frowned. 'He should have thought of that before running his mouth, shouldn't he?'

Jaja said, 'If he be my servant, I would have to crush him for his insolence.'

'I could provide you with servants, if you need any,' Brathwaite said.

'No. But thank you. I made arrangement a'ready through the Governor. It was meant to be done before I come. Yesterday, I ate with Governor and his wife. He says my servants to come by weekend.'

'Oh,' Brathwaite said sourly. He turned toward Becka. 'Prepare one of the bedrooms for me, Becka. I'll sit up in one of the meeting rooms for a while, but will retire soon. I've had a long day.'

CHAPTER EIGHT

The First Secretary arrived early next morning to accompany Jaja to the Assembly Chambers. Mr. Brathwaite had already left for the city in his carriage. Becka was doing her chores. Jaja, watching from the second-floor window as he saw the Secretary's carriage pull into the yard, adjusted his European jacket and went down the stairs. He'd been sixty-seven when the British had put him on trial. At that age, he'd been stronger and quicker than most men half his age, and feared by many. From the moment he heard the sentence of exile in that airless room in Accra, he'd begun to feel his age. But while his gait was slower than in his African glory days, he felt healthier and happier now than at any time since his arrival in the West Indies. In about two years, he could return, to pick up from where he'd left off. He'd recently received word from his chiefs through his British trader-friend, Mr. Miller, that British supercargoes had set up palm-oil trading posts in Opobo, had cut out the African middlemen, and had threatened to destroy Opobo if the chiefs would not cooperate. Jaja felt rage at this further news of Britain's arrogance and the loss of his markets. They were the criminals, not he. The thought of one day securing justice burned inside him. He would slaughter every last one of them and drink their blood from a gourd. These thoughts burned as he approached the First Secretary who was waiting in one of the meeting rooms.

The official rose from his chair like a pole. His loosely-fitting gaberdine pants and tweed jacket were sharply pressed, the chain from the pocket-watch competing with his boot buckles in its shine. He acknowledged Jaja with a nod and gestured towards the door. Jaja nodded, wondering why the rush, and followed him outside to the carriage.

The sky was cloudless and crisp like a sheet of flat blue glass. Jaja breathed in the fresh morning air tinged with the smell of mint floating in from the herb garden at the side of the house. The crowing cocks reminded him again of home, of the day's announcements, of duties to perform. Loss lanced him. Oh to be dressed in kingly garments, cane in hand, rolled goatskin mat under his arm on the way to visit his chiefs in the court house to discuss the town's affairs; or entering one of his wife's huts where his grandchildren bucked like lambs and squealed in glee; or joining a gathering in his or someone else's compound, the kola nut broken by the eldest person and passed around in order of seniority. Kola nut and alligator pepper. Kola nut and bitter nut. Kola nut and palm wine.

The First Secretary's voice broke his reverie. 'How is your accommodation? The Governor expresses his wish that you are as comfortable as possible in your new residence.'

'It be nice place,' Jaja replied. 'The cocks at home crow the same.'

The First Secretary straightened his collar nervously at Jaja's enigmatic reply. 'Well, if you are in need of anything, let me know, and I will do my best to accommodate your request.'

The carriage approached the Wharfside, circled the statue of Lord Nelson, and made a left turn into the courtyard of the public buildings which now housed Parliament. The First Secretary told Jaja these had been completed in 1871; before that parliament was held in public houses such as the Roebuck Tavern. The buildings both impressed and depressed Jaja. They radiated British power, the country he'd once loved but now despised.

The First Secretary led the king up the four flights of winding wooden stairs to the public gallery, and ushered him into a front seat with a panoramic view of the proceedings below. Soon, the bewigged Marshall of the Assembly appeared, carrying the mace which he laid on two wooden blocks. When Jaja looked more closely, he saw something familiar about the Marshall's burly physique. As he turned, Jaja recognized the heavy jaws and pink almost feminine lips of Cheeseman Moe Brathwaite, owner of Walmer Cottage and Jordans Plantation. Why had Brathwaite not mentioned his official position?

The Secretary saw the surprised look on Jaja's face and smiled.

With the mace in place, the Speaker opened the proceedings. There was something familiar to Jaja about the way the Speaker and an Anglican priest took their seats in high-backed chairs. The speaker's was inside a throne-like wooden booth with an etching of the scales of justice and the British coat of arms at its top, like some red, white, and blue bird.

The priest rose and said, 'Let us all stand.' The rustle of swizzle-tailed suits whispered like surf. He prayed for the island's leaders, asking that 'wisdom and understanding lead to what is just, so that *Your* will be done, O Lord.'

The Speaker then said in a grave voice, 'I move the proceedings of the House be open.' Jaja recognised the tone that he used to set the mood of a meeting. The robed, bewigged Speaker even sat like a chief or king, his feet flat to the ground and his knees spread wide apart like a fan.

A member shot up, the tips of his hands resting on the table before him.

'The Honourable Member, Mr. Moore,' the Speaker said.

'Mr. Speaker, I move this resolution with its proposals to counter the lingering ill effects of the 1884 depression upon the labouring classes. We're still feeling the aftershocks of the plunge in London's sugar prices, and it doesn't seem as if it will abate even after these seven long years. Our profitability has been considerably reduced. There is talk of Britain appointing a commission to investigate this state of affairs, not only here but in all of its West Indian colonies, and to make appropriate recommendations.'

Jaja scanned the chamber which was empty save for the members of the Executive Council who made up the Lower House of Assembly. Some of them shuffled their files; others appeared to read intently from documents before them; still others pulled their chins or noses or passed hands over their foreheads. One member appeared to be fast asleep. From time to time, the First Secretary leaned over to explain how parliament was organized. Jaja learnt that the Upper Chamber, not meeting today, contained the legislative arm of the government; its members were wholly nominated by other elected members. This was in contrast to the assembly members who were nominated by the

Governor. This was puzzling, but as Jaja listened to the debates, some sense of what was going on formed in his mind.

Another member said, 'The lower classes are exacerbating our already stressed circumstances by squatting on land in the Scotland highlands districts to grow ground provisions. If something is not done, we will lose our labour force.'

'We are going to have to make a concession for our own survival,' another said. 'The unrest of the lower class of workers grows worse each year. We can diversify our crops and survive in spite of the poor returns from sugar, but their unrest represents an even more sinister state of affairs – threatens our extermination. We cannot allow this to happen.'

Another member said, 'We know that some behind the Commission want to break up the estates and support the peasantry in gaining proprietary rights. We can fight if we like, but I say, "Let the night come." I am convinced it is better to let the lower classes have the illusion of progress than retiring to bed in fear of having my throat cut before morning. Have members forgotten what transpired in Leers just last week?'

The First Secretary whispered that there had been unrest at Leers Plantation when a female house servant, alleging sexual assault on the part of the owner, had attempted to kill the entire household by poisoning their tea. She'd enlisted the help of one of the plantation's cane cutters, a man named Solomon, who was ready to slit any throats that survived the poisoning.

Jaja looked around the hall, at the rows of wooden desks at which the members were seated, at the windows surrounding the hall with their green wooden louvres. At the top of each of the twelve arched windows was a crown-shaped stained-glass panel picturing British politicians and monarchs. Jaja asked whose was the image in the arch immediately to their left. It was Oliver Cromwell. Jaja studied the image and, though it was cast only in profile, he thought he saw some slant of cruelty in the patrician nose and thin mouth. Jaja didn't need to ask whose image hung directly above the Speaker's seat and he felt rage swell inside him as he studied the portrait of Queen Victoria.

'Are you all right, Jaja?' The First Secretary had heard the king's involuntary groan. Jaja did not reply.

'I'll never agree to government purchase of my lands – to be divided up and sold to support peasant agriculture!' a House member was saying. 'There is no guarantee that the insatiable lower classes will be satisfied with these reforms. Nothing we do will please them – barring giving them our heads on a platter!'

'Nonsense! Slavery has long been over. We shouldn't fear violence now,' a lone member retorted.

The assembly continued in this vein until a group of black Barbadians came into the gallery. They gathered in the seats surrounding Jaja, staring and beaming at him. One or two even went up to touch him. They were not interested in the proceedings below. They had come to see the flesh-and-blood king they'd heard was in the House. Some could not restrain themselves from making comment, and their voices grew louder.

'Please! Please!' The Speaker sounded his gavel. 'I will have to clear the gallery. Please!'

But the word was out. More people came into the gallery to see the king. Jaja felt an uplift in his spirit as if he were a soaring bird.

'Order! Order! Officers, clear the gallery!'

The Speaker concluded, 'I move the proceedings of the House be suspended until one-thirty!'

Jaja had a smile on his face, the kind he wore when he emerged from one of his wife's huts, or he'd resolved a difficult trade dispute or gained some new knowledge about life. From boyhood, he'd craved knowledge and that hunger never left him. Perhaps it was this desire for learning that had led him into a relationship with the British – but why had he let down his guard and believed the promises of protection they had offered him? Yet, he had to admire them, foul breakers of oaths that they were, for the scale and thoroughness with which they carried out their business.

As they walked across the courtyard, squinting in the midday sun, the First Secretary asked Jaja what he thought of the discussions.

'They be very good. But it seem members upset over support of de peasant proprietary rights.' Jaja had long decided it was best to be agreeable around his captors and hedge his verbal engagements with them. He'd made a slip at the Governor's luncheon, but would be more careful in future. He would be cryptic and non-committal. He'd always watched and listened much more than he spoke, a quality which he relied on even more heavily in his exile. He kept his open conversations for Becka, and looked forward to her company again and hearing how Mr. Brathwaite had resolved the matter of the carriage and ice fees.

The carriage took them through the north gate of the Parliament building, going left on Marhill Street. Market people had come to him in the House, and Jaja felt a bond with the vendors they passed, their trays fastened atop wooden barrels, brimming with fruits and vegetables. At Magazine Lane, the huckster presence suddenly ended, and a right turn onto Pinfold Street revealed Central Hotel midway up on the right side of the road, where Jaja and the First Secretary now headed.

The dining room was filled with clerks in white shirts and dark ties, and one or two women with their beaux seizing the brief opportunity for courtship. Jaja noted that the servers and bartenders were the only ones in the room who looked like him.

Not long after they'd been seated, a group of four men approached the table. The First Secretary rose from his seat. 'Reverend Henry, it's a pleasure to see you again.'

The clerical gentleman said, 'And so soon at that.'

'Would you gentlemen care to join us? We do have enough chairs.'

When everyone was seated, the First Secretary continued. 'Your sermon at St. Cyprian's last Sunday was very good indeed, a blessing to me and my family… Please, may I introduce you to our visitor, King Jaja. He's here as a guest of the Crown. You might have read of his visit in the *Herald*.' The men smiled in a way that indicated they'd heard nothing of the king.

One said, 'We just arrived on the island yesterday.' The First Secretary informed Jaja that these gentlemen were Wesleyan ministers in the island for their annual conference. Jaja nodded and smiled. He shook the hand of the minister to his immediate right and nodded to the other three. He was thinking about the Wesleyan missionaries whom he'd mistakenly allowed to build a church in Opobo. His concern over the collapse of his society had cost him many sleepless nights, but he'd fought back. He'd often told the missionaries, 'I want all my people to saby book.' They had been encouraged by this, only to be disappointed when he set up his own school without any Christian activity. He was very fond of reading, especially about natural history, and he was happy to use whatever European technology aided his people's progress. He had acquired gunboats and Gatling guns from freelance European traders. Weapons such as these ensured he could suppress any civil strife in his kingdom.

The waiter reached Jaja. He ordered lamb with boiled English potatoes, fried plantain, and greens.

Jaja asked the men where they were staying.

'Right here at this hotel,' one of them said. 'It is most commodious. We always stay here when we come to this beautiful island.'

Another of the clergymen asked Jaja, 'Is it right for a man to have more than one wife in Africa?'

'I am an old man now,' Jaja said. 'You had better ask my son.'

The First Secretary's lips twitched with suppressed laughter, and he looked at Jaja with a trace of admiration.

Lunch over, the two men continued along Pinfold Street and on to Roebuck Street. Jaja was beginning to tire, although he had felt well all morning. He had brought his iron-wood cane with him but had not used it. But when the First Secretary said he had to make a stop at Central Ice House to deliver a letter to Whitfield, Jaja groaned silently. Then he recalled the ice house's owner's threat to increase the rental for his carriage, and he wanted a resolution to that dispute. He had hardly spoken to Becka since Brathwaite had come and knew she was anxious over the matter.

The ice house stood at a corner of Roebuck Street, its coral-stone façade dingy with dust, its once green louvred windows cobwebbed between the slats. Along with ice, it dealt in groceries and fresh meat – where Worrell got most of Walmer Cottage's supplies. A marked-out space at the side of the building facilitated the easy loading of the ice which came down a chute right into a cart below. While Jaja waited for the First Secretary to return, a thin man with slightly bent shoulders came up to the carriage and introduced himself as John Cheeks.

'You must be King Jaja,' he said. Cheeks stood tall, even with his hunched shoulders, an energetic man, probably in his thirties, with wide-spaced, sparkling eyes and brushed-back, sleek brown hair.

'Yes. I be Jaja.' He reached down to shake the man's proffered hand. Cheeks introduced himself as Mr. Whitfield's clerk. He'd begun as a boy running errands, had progressed to shelf-packer, cashier and, finally, accounts clerk. He recounted this story like someone speaking not of himself but of his offspring.

Jaja said, 'As my nurse Becka says, "If crab don' walk 'bout, 'e don' get fat." Those who stay at home accomplish nothing. I too am a living example of hard work. I like that in a man.'

'You should know Mr. Brathwaite's man, Worrell, has been telling us how you want to make him your slave because you are an African king. He makes you out to be a devil, but I can see, already, you are not. You are nothing at all like he portrayed you.'

'Worrell is an insolent man. He has no manners. But he won't be at Mr. Brathwaite's much longer. I will have my own servants soon.'

Just then the First Secretary and Mr. Whitfield came out of the building. The First Secretary introduced Jaja.

'The king?' Mr. Whitfield said this with what appeared to be a disbelieving smile. 'Do you find the Victoria to your liking?'

The temptation to say that he loathed the Victoria (meaning the Queen) came to Jaja's lips. Instead, he said, 'The carriage is to my liking. I like how it ride and hope to take it out to the country in a few days.'

John Cheeks looked at Jaja curiously. He pursed his lips and nodded to Jaja, who nodded back, and thoughtfully watched Cheeks go up the steps of the building.

Whitfield said, 'What you felt, Jaja, is the effects of a full suspension spring. Second to none and guaranteed for a smooth ride.'

CHAPTER NINE

Next day, the First Secretary took the king to visit the city stores. When the driver had parked in the Public Buildings courtyard, the First Secretary said, 'You have the bearing of a true statesman, a man of honour. I will run some of my own errands and meet you back here around one-thirty?'

'Thank you,' Jaja said, and they shook hands.

The First Secretary added, 'I have to meet someone for lunch at twelve, Jaja. So you can eat with me at Central Hotel… or perhaps you might enjoy buying from one of the vendors. You can't get a better taste of Barbados food than from a sidewalk vendor.'

Jaja understood and appreciated the official's discretion. Taking his cane from the carriage, he adjusted his felt hat and politely bade the First Secretary goodbye.

This was the first time in the later years of his confinement that he'd been allowed to go anywhere alone. As he left the courtyard's western gate and breathed deep the mid-morning air he thought of Opobo, his sons Sunday and Saturday, his chiefs, his wives. He thought of Emma who had so steadfastly supported him during the years of conflict with the British consuls – first, Hewitt, then the malicious Harry Johnson, breaker of oaths, the one directly responsible for his demise. Sorrow began to nudge him. To keep it at bay, he turned his thoughts to Becka, her care, her caresses, her songs. Jaja was so deep in thought, he was hardly aware he'd reached Roebuck Street and was standing at the foot of the coral-stone steps of Central Ice House. And there, almost as if he was expecting him, was John Cheeks, nattily dressed in a white jacket, striped tie and dark gabardines.

'I come to town to see shops and say I stop by your place to visit,' Jaja said.

'I'm glad you did, Mr. Jaja. It is good to see you again.' They shook hands. Cheeks' wide eyes shone.

'There is something I want to discuss with you, Mr. Cheeks. Or rather, information I wish to share with you. We speak privately?'

Cheeks was silent for a moment. 'Have you finished looking at the shops?'

'No, I have not yet been.'

'Well, you could visit the shops on Roebuck and meet me back here around eleven-thirty. That's when I take my lunch. We could talk then.'

'Good. Thank you,' Jaja said.

Inside a clothing store, he frowned as he looked at the all-British items on display. From his readings of Caribbean island history, he knew that the black inhabitants of the islands had originated from West Africa, and the recognisable traces he saw on so many faces made him sure that many had been brought here from Nigeria. They had lost their freedom, their African languages, and had been forced to wear the tattered clothing once worn by the planter and merchant families, since there was no way for them to acquire African fabrics. Those ragged clothes would have first been sold to the planter and merchant classes from a store like this one. Then a horrified thought came to him. Had some of the prisoners caught in inter-tribal wars or skirmishes and sold to households in his region been, in turn, sold to the supercargoes on the coast? In 1828, he himself had been snatched when he was seven and sold to a Bonny household, twenty-one years after the British slave trade had been formally abolished. He'd obtained his freedom when he was twenty-one because of his talent for trading. From older people in his Bonny household he'd heard of others, slaves like himself, who had been sold to Europeans. This would explain why some of their fellow slaves would sometimes suddenly disappear, never to be seen again. Now he was suffering a similar fate, and the irony did not escape him. He'd avoided being illegally sold to Spanish or Portuguese slave traders as a youth; now here he was, a king of a sovereign country, in illegal bondage.

The female clerk, who had retreated into a back room of the store when Jaja entered, now re-emerged with a middle-aged man who approached Jaja and asked if he needed help.

'No,' Jaja said. 'I just looking around.'

'Perhaps you might try the Broad Street stores,' the man said. 'They have a much wider selection of items.' Jaja could see the store-owner's discomfort. This amused him and he very deliberately walked around the store a second time, carefully examining the hats and bonnets, the artificial flowers and ornaments, the men's tweeds and flannels, the boots and shoes. He finally nodded to the now flushed owner and slowly left the store, adjusting his hat and tapping his iron-wood cane.

He browsed a few more shops and then stopped by a roadside vendor whose trays were bursting with an assortment of fruits and ground provisions. He recognized most of them and stared intently at the yams. Not only did they feed the people of his beloved country, but yams could make a man wealthy and respected. Of all the festivals celebrated in Opobo, it was the New Yam Festival he most missed. He purchased a few yams – bulbous, stout, dark brown, with fibrous root hairs long as a man's beard. With his bag of provisions he returned to Central Ice House.

'I must return to courtyard by one-thirty,' he told John Cheeks as they left the building. Cheeks had relieved himself of the white jacket he wore inside the building, revealing a white, long-sleeved shirt.

'Don't worry, Jaja. We have more than enough time. It's now just after eleven-thirty, and it's a short walk to our hotel on Pinfold Street.'

'Our hotel?'

'Yes, Mr. Whitfield owns both businesses.'

'Yes, I notice they carry same first names, and I did wonder.'

At Central, John Cheeks requested a private upstairs dining room.

When they were seated, Jaja said, 'I believe you are Scottish from your name and speech?'

'Yes. How do you know that?'

'I have very good trader friend who speaks as you,' Jaja said.

Then, his voice low but hard, he added, 'We share a common grievance... you and I. The cruelty of the English.'

'You're very perceptive, Jaja,' Cheeks said. 'I'm not at all fond of the English, and, yes, this all stems from my Scottish roots. They treated us... shall I say... criminally. Where do I start?... Over two hundred years ago, Cromwell sent thousands of my people to the West Indies with only the clothes on their backs. My great-great-great-great grandfather was one of the hundreds sent to Barbados, one of the Covenanters whom Cromwell regarded as a traitor. Came with nothing save the kilt he was wearing. That's why they called us "Red Legs". Put to labour and scorched red out there in those fields.' His voice lowered to a whisper. 'He didn't survive the climate, my ancestor. By twenty-six, he was dead, with a wife and four children.'

'What "crime" was he suppose to commit?'

'He supported the 1638 Scottish Covenant in protesting against changes that made the English king head of the Church. The Covenanters felt that only Jesus Christ should be the head of the church. For a time they were in alliance with Cromwell, then they fell out. The Covenanters were defeated and many sent here. We call that period "The Killing Times".'

Jaja grunted in sympathy, shaking his head as Cheeks spoke. He was sure this was a man he could trust.

'The British want to kill me,' Jaja said. 'They take everything I own, my markets and my freedom. They say I break treaty, their Mimina Agreement. Their claim to being Protectorate of Delta say my place lost its sovereignty. I ignore them. I be sovereign king. So they lure me to boat on pretext of settling palaver...'

'Palaver?'

'...Yes, settle dispute between us. They sentence me at mock trial in Accra with a jury of all Englishmen: five years exile and fine of five thousand pounds. You know the rest.'

Cheeks shook his head from side to side and said, 'The English... How might I assist you, Jaja?'

'I must get out of island. I must get back to my people. Can you help me?'

CHAPTER TEN

Becka hummed as she prepared two sets of dinners. More even than the feel of Bajan sunlight and wind on her face, the melodies of the folk songs that rose spontaneously inside her made her feel alive. One meal, of Yorkshire pudding, was for Mr. Brathwaite and herself; she expected him to stay overnight again. The other meal was for Jaja. She had kept him on a strict diet since his arrival: in the morning, oatmeal sprinkled with Indian jujube, what she called dunks, and chia to calm his nervous system, warm milk and honeyed bread, and lettuce juice flavoured with lemon. Usually, she'd make a soup for him around lunchtime of boiled or steamed leafy vegetables with fish, mushrooms and generous sprinklings of dill and basil. Day after day, she witnessed his returning strength, and she saw the steady gleam in his eyes as they settled on her.

It was uncanny, but she felt she had known Jaja for so much longer than she actually did. At first this sensation had startled her, but she was coming to accept it as her destiny. But was she taking advantage of a sick man? Things had happened so quickly between them. Was he serious about taking her to Opobo? Was he just lonely, missing his wife-to-be who had remained in St. Vincent? When his exile ended, would he just stop off in St. Vincent to collect his wife and return with her to his kingdom across the seas? These questions wouldn't go away, but something was happening, some extraordinary thing that might take them beyond their individual motives, stations, backgrounds and ages. But was there a mutual future?

She continued humming as she attended to Jaja's meal. When she uncovered the pot of beans and rice, she saw a few tiny volcanoes on its surface from whose craters steam softly hissed and gurgled. She closed the lid and moved the pot from the fire; it would now cook with its own heat. With an approving hand, she prodded the chicken Worrell had killed, plucked, and brought to her a few hours earlier. It sat in a large bowl on the counter top and would be stewed and served with lettuce and peanuts.

Around three-thirty Becka heard Mr. Brathwaite's carriage roll into the driveway. He seemed a decent person after all, involving her in conversation, requesting she called him Mr. Brathwaite and not Sir. She no longer feared him behaving inappropriately. Besides, the Governor's guards were always there. Jaja was there. Yet, suddenly, a hidden fish of doubt darted to the surface of her mind. Could the presence of the guards be the only reason for his good behaviour? What if the guards weren't there? Would she be in danger? Patsy's stories still ran deep inside her. She could never really trust any whiteman member of the ruling class. Never.

'Well, I have good news at last,' Mr. Brathwaite said. 'News that will make you happy, Becka.'

'Yes, Mr. Brathwaite?'

'Mr. Whitfield finally backed down from his threat to raise the rental fee on Jaja's carriage. But this was only after I threatened to rent from someone else. So Worrell can count his lucky stars. I won't have to let him go.'

'I glad to hear that. I glad everything work out fuh ev'rybody.'

'What are you making for dinner today, Becka?'

'Yorkshire pudding.'

'My favourite,' Mr. Brathwaite said. He had a thin, straight auburn moustache that grew even straighter as he smiled.

'You want a cup of tea, Mr. Brathwaite?'

'Yes, that would be delightful, Becka. I'll be reading in one of the public rooms. And by the way, I'll be heading back to Jordans tomorrow morning now that my business in the city has been resolved. And further… Whitfield has reduced the weekly cost of ice by a few shillings.'

'Very good, Mr. Brathwaite. I happy fo' you.'

Becka was thinking how glad she was Worrell hadn't lost his job, when the carriage carrying Jaja and the government official pulled in. She put the kettle on to boil, briskly wiped her hands on her apron, and went to the south-side door. She waved as the carriage slowly passed, Jaja smiling broadly. Mr. Brathwaite would be leaving in the morning. She and Jaja would be alone again.

She took the bag of yams from Jaja when he and the government man reached the door. The latter said to Becka, 'If you would be so kind, I would like to have a word with Mr. Brathwaite.'

'Yes, Sir. I tell him you hey.' When she returned, Becka led the First Secretary to the public room where Mr. Brathwaite was still engrossed in *The Barbados Herald*, his feet stretched out on an ottoman. Becka found Jaja in one of the other public rooms reclining on a mahogany divan.

'Jaja, you tired. Come and go in you bed. I goin' call you when you dinner ready. Got something real good fo' you.'

'I know, me girl. I know, me dove,' Jaja said, looking up at her with both hunger and fatigue.

After Jaja's nap, Becka sat with him in one of the public rooms. He told her about the shops he'd visited on Roebuck Street, of the luncheon at Central Hotel. There was something else he had to tell her, but that would have to wait until Mr. Brathwaite returned to Jordan's. Becka wondered what it was that couldn't be spoken about now, but the look of animation on Jaja's face and the urgency in his voice betrayed that it was something significant. She told him about Mr. Brathwaite's resolution of the dispute with Whitfield over the carriage fees and that he was expected to return to St. George in the morning. Worrell would keep his handyman's job. Jaja frowned, but said nothing. Becka really wished the two of them could get along. She'd told Jaja she liked Worrell as a friend and the king had respected that sentiment, but only because of her. There was no respect between the two men, and Becka knew there would be none unless Worrell abandoned his hope of involvement with her. Jaja could not be fooled. He would have heard the passionate tone in Worrell's greetings and seen his lingering looks.

CHAPTER ELEVEN

Although Becka's care had increased the quality of his rest, Jaja still occasionally suffered from insomnia. That night was one of those times. Past and future flicker through his mind.

His son, Sunday, is on the coronation stool after Opobo's two years in the dark forest. Trade continues as before, his middlemen still operating between hinterland oil suppliers and European supercargoes on the coast. Sunday thwarts the consuls' push into the hinterlands. The British African Association surrenders its hinterland trading posts for 500 puncheons each and promises to stay on the coast. *Do not believe them as I did, Sunday. Do not believe one word of the British. Their word means nothing. If they comply now, they will come back again with more guns and winking eyes.*

A British consul is now a bird of control over Opobo town in civil and criminal matters. Offences are reported to and investigated by him, even petty disagreements between people. He now has power to impose fines or sentence with terms of imprisonment. Appeals against a judgment are winged to the Consul General at Calabar for confirmation, amendment or annulment. Jaja is happy to see that the Native Authority has not been dismantled, that traditional religious festivals are held and masks performed – the masquerade club, the Owuogwu, at the fore. Along with its cultural and ancestral representations, the Owuogwu still retains traditional judicial power in disputes such as those involving runaway wives, and the market-master still enforces the market rules. The chiefs-in-council still have a role to play in Opobo's affairs, still make judgments announced to the public by the Owuogwu. He remembers back to a time when Europe's religious zeal is strong but African followers were sparse and inconsequential.

Jaja's thoughts twist and arc another thirty years. It is August, and he is in his compound. Rain clouds build but no-one wants to come inside the rooms that line the compound's inner walls. His grandchildren scamper about and even at this early age they know they must not step on the boundary line of the compound's entrance. They must step over it with sandals off. They must step over the crosspieces of the wide, cool porches so as not to offend the ancestors. There's an old many-roomed building with an *ala-umi* near the centre of the compound and his reception room sprouts from the building with its baobab wood posts and corrugated iron sheets. There in the middle of his compound, he reclines in his grand upstairs house that's raised off the earth on tall iron and wooden poles, underneath which the women dry the clothes during the rainy season. Right now, young girls are performing this task, as the clouds darken. Soon, he will upgrade his house, using either brick or cement blocks, with a European-styled exterior. At the back of the dwelling houses, near the river, the large open sheds house his war canoes, expertly crafted from a single log, seven feet wide by over sixty feet long. His own war canoe, *The Queen*, is there. He thinks he should have named it *My Queen*, after his first wife Osunju, for any echo of that other queen, Victoria, kills his joy.

Outside the compound, other homes and buildings used to be formed by the embrace of mud and wattle. Recently he'd seen muscular young men bring zinc sheets to the site in canoes and seen dwellings rise with roofs of metal corrugations. He notes how some rust and fall. It wasn't always this way!

His fears leap forward. Chukwu, what has happened? What has happened to his place? The untended woodwork rots and decays. Broken window panes are unmended. Soon the rain will beat in to spoil the furniture and floor.

Decay finds his compound. The reception room collapses, the floor sunken like a mud hammock. Broken glass and dampness are everywhere, dampness that destroys the decorations and English-made furnishings. Dirt and dust cover everything, including the large banquet tables he used when he entertained the European traders. His chairs are sagging and broken, their beautifully embroidered cloth coverings faded, mildewed, motheaten. Photographs of his European friends and son Sunday, taken in England, have bleached and faded. The coronation stool, to be sat on only by an *amanyanabo*, has been half-eaten by insects. Carved ivory horns, emblems of his dynasty, are heaped like discarded rubbish in a corner along with old rusty trunks overflowing with neglected letters and papers.

And grief of griefs, what has happened to the ancestral shrines in their lofty rooms with wide entrances? O Chukwu! Chukwu! The large roof beams, to which lines of animal skulls were tied, and the tall altars are falling down. Fragments of china lie on the floor, reminders of the British who dined in his banquet halls and who exchanged gifts with him. One Toby jug is intact, its heavy-jowled, jovial subject, in long coat and tricorn hat, holds his mug of beer in one hand and a tobacco pipe in the other. Drums and headdresses for ceremonies and masks lie in corners and in sacks hanging from the walls. Everything is cloaked with cobwebs, soot and dust. The chief shrine of the town, located in what is now a decaying building in the corrugated-covered market, houses an old insect-eaten carving of Asimiri, the founder of Bonny, which Jaja brought from that town, along with two ancient stools and an Ijaw-styled headdress. There are discarded water-spirit headdresses, part-human, part-fish, others part-human, part-animal, the flattened human face on the top facing the sky with a ram's horns sprouting out, or the spiked bill of a swordfish, or the jaw of a hippopotamus, or the head of a snake, bird, crocodile or tortoise. He was the crocodile, over six feet tall, who walked on human legs with feathers, bells, mirrors, and brightly-coloured kinte cloth.

This is what he feared and now fears more than ever: his people's confusion of who they are. Hypocritical Christians have taken over his people's culture and they no longer recognise themselves. Some worship two gods, the Christian god and the god of their fathers. They are neutered, split down the middle, staring blindly to the heavens. The Owuogbo Society is no more. No more their masquerades, the ripple and smoke of the ancestral spirits billowing from their heads. He'd hoped they might join together the two worlds, but never for his people to lose their traditional beliefs. Why shouldn't his people perform their traditional plays during the Christian festivals? Bridge the two worlds, but at all costs never forfeit their traditional culture.

All the colonials wanted was our palm oil. That's all they ever wanted, to make candles and perfumed soaps and cosmetics. They built public latrines on rickety posts over the water-edge of my Imo River. My people's self-esteem is dead. Even if they sweep their wattle and mud homes and keep paths neat and ditches clear, they're no longer interested in the craft of making things – just fishing implements, straw hats, a little cotton weaving. They do their little fishing, selling vegetables, fruits, and clothing in the market shed, buying what they cannot produce with the few manillas they get from selling the little they produce. One shilling to six manillas – I want them stop accepting British currency to preserve our nationhood. Now, I see my body turned to bronze, fixed on a grey granite plinth with an inscribed marble base and surrounded by an iron railing. I carry my staff. I carry my rolled goatskin mat. In front of the iron rails, on the neatly-edged grass, four ebony goats curl in sleep. I'm history.

It was not until about two o'clock in the morning that he finally fell asleep. And even as he slept, he twisted and arced like a panicked fish struggling in the nets of the present and the future.

CHAPTER TWELVE

After breakfast, the king went to one of the public rooms to read. The First Secretary had recently arranged for all three of the island's newspapers to be sent to Walmer Cottage: *The Barbados Globe*, *The Barbados Herald* and *The Barbados Times*. These papers carried no engraved illustrations and comprised mainly rehashed news from England, local political and social news, and advertisements. Some back issues of the papers were also sent to the king and it was in one of these, *The Herald*, that he'd read of how, "at the Governor's residence and in the presence of two ladies, the poor king requested four legs of mutton which he fully devoured." He was not amused by this ridiculous exaggeration. The lamb was very tasty, it was true, and he remembered requesting a second serving of it, but who could possibly eat four legs of lamb?

He heard the sounds of Mr. Brathwaite's carriage dying away as it left for St. George. Shortly afterward, Becka came into greet him with a hug and a kiss.

'Me dove, me queen.'

Becka was about to sit on his lap, but Jaja held her by the waist and guided her onto the chair's arm.

'Sorry, Jaja. I forget 'bout you knee.'

Jaja smiled and shook his head slowly from side to side, remembering how terribly they'd ached when he first arrived. He looked at Becka and said, 'You hand healing me.'

Just then, there was a loud knock on the side door, and Becka went to see who was there. She returned to Jaja and said, 'A man out dey fo' you.'

A lanky man, barefooted, and dressed in clean but worn cotton shirt and gabardines stood there.

He said, 'I name Phillips. De Guv'nor send me to work fuh you. I can do some o' everything.' His unusually long arms hung at his sides until he extended one of them to hold out a letter.

'I be expecting two of you,' Jaja said tearing open the letter. 'Where is my other servant?'

Phillips looked perplexed, awkwardly clasping his hands behind his back.

Becka said, 'Jaja, ask the guv'ment man when he come, or ride over to de guv'nor and ask he. You should know de main roads good by now.'

Jaja folded and pocketed the note and informed Phillips of his duties, stressing that none of them would involve work inside the house, except on the occasion of any indoor carpentry repairs. He was to take care of the carriage, horses and cow, bathe his dog weekly, and be generally available to do any errands requested either by himself or Becka.

'How to address you, Suh? I hear you is a king.'

Jaja smiled and said, 'Mr. Jaja be good.'

'Yes, Suh, Mr. Jaja,' Phillips said, and left for the sheds to check on the animals.

Turning to Becka, the king said, 'I want teach you a game. It is game my generals and me play before war. It sharpen us. Help with strategy. I go back up to get it and we play on bench in the garden.'

'Awright. I wait hey fuh you.'

With Oko Jumbo running ahead, Jaja and Becka soon reached the eastern fringe of the property, noting as they passed Neptune's alabaster lily pot, a mahogany's flaking trunk and a flamboyant's bloody effulgence.

Jaja had brought the iron-wood warri gameboard with him into exile. In St. Vincent, he'd play by himself or with local residents whom he'd befriended. He was determined to stay alert, to keep his mind sharp. He had to be prepared for his eventual return to Opobo, to assume his duties as *amanyanabo*, the people's king.

Jaja laid the board down on the bench and took out the wooden pieces from the pocket of his kente dashiki. He and Becka twisted round to face each other. Oko Jumbo curled at his master's feet.

Jaja placed four seeds in each of the board's twelve receptacles. He called the circular containers houses. He said, 'I have six on my side. You six. It's a game of war. I try capture plenty your seeds. Whoever capture twenty-five first, win game.'

Becka said, 'Suppose all-we capture twenty-four. Wha' we do then?'

'Then nobody a-win. It would draw.'

They decided who was to make the first play by Jaja picking up a seed, putting his hands behind his back and secretly switching the seed from hand to hand, then bringing each clenched hand forward, arms crossed, and asking Becka to guess which hand contained the seed. She touched the left fist.

'No, me girl. I get to play.' Jaja lifted all the seeds from one of his houses and sowed them, one in each house to the right of the house from which he'd played. The last seed landed in the second house on Becka's side of the board. Becka then made the identical play and they continued in this vein. At one point Becka's last sown seed landed in a house on Jaja's side that contained only two seeds.

'You can capture me,' Jaja said laughing. 'You do well. You take advantage of my weak house. You capture when your last seed fall on house with just one or two seeds in it.'

The game reached a point where Becka had only one seed in the second house on her side of the board and Jaja held a house with the same number of seeds in it. If Jaja had made the move, Becka would have been without any seeds to play, and she would have forfeited all of the remaining seeds on the board.

'De British would do well to learn warri. It teach to play fair. It teach no unfair competition and punish the man who do it.' So Jaja refrained from capturing Becka's last seed. Instead, he pulled the eight seeds from his third house and sowed them one by one to the right, so that five of them were placed on Becka's side of the game board. Only her sixth house was empty now. The war game was now an open contest once more.

'I have made new friend,' Jaja began.

Becka cast a puzzled look at the king.

'His name is John Cheeks from Central Ice House. He is a sympathizer.'

'He black or white?'

'He is white man.'

'You better be careful, Jaja. Wuh' he say?'

'He will help. He will help us leave the island and go back to my country.'

'I told you I cyan leave wid you, Jaja. I cyan leave my sister to look after we mudder all by she self. Dah is why I tek this job hey, to make a few shillings a week to help tek care o' she.'

'I know, me dove. But I will send for you when I reach Opobo, if you can come at that time.'

Jaja told her of the plan to escape on a cargo vessel going to South Carolina and from there he would make his way back to Africa. John was expected to visit him this evening to update him on what, if any, progress had been made.

'I frighten fo' you, Jaja. I don't want nothing happen to you. You trust white people? Suppose he turn on you?'

'I make good white trading friends in Opobo, especially Mr. Miller who right now is facilitating my business in Opobo Town. He arrange oil shipments for me to England in exchange for such things as parts, powder, gin, and casks of salt.'

'But dis is Buhbados. You t'ink de white people here sweet?'

'I no trust most white people. Trusting their word bring a-plenty trouble, the reason you see me here now. That is more reason I have to get back to my place. To put disgrace on Her Majesty. She give me Sword of Honour, yet deny me my freedom, my markets, my country.'

'Bajan white people would bath in Victoria bath water, yuh hear? Dah is why I 'fraid fo' you, Jaja. You sure you can trust dis John Cheeks?'

'I be desperate, me dove. I must trust someone. What have I more to lose?'

'They could hang you if you get ketch.'

'I take my chances.' Jaja said. 'He be Scottish. The English played them dirty too. That man name Cromwell. Before they enslave your people, they send Scottish people here to work like slaves for them. John, like me and you, have strong reason to hate England.'

★

When Becka brought John Cheeks into the public room that

evening, Jaja saw her carefully examining him from head to foot to see if there was any treachery hiding there. Under the intensity of her surveillance Cheeks clasped and unclasped his hands, puckered his nose and blushed. Jaja suggested to John that they take a stroll in the garden.

Cheeks seemed to take the surroundings for granted, but Jaja had fallen in love with the casuarina, flamboyants, yellow frangipani, crotons, bougainvillea, silk cotton, and baobab trees. The mild breezes dancing over them transported him back to Opobo, and the masquerade colours of the garden ignited his spirits just as the music of the birds inspired his hopes. But it was Becka who had touched his mind and body in the most marvellous way. The thought made him look back, but they had already walked too far from the yard to see her.

Cheeks said, 'There is a vessel that makes a trip to the United States every two months. To South Carolina. I can get you on that steamer, but not as who you are.'

Jaja looked puzzled. 'What do you mean?'

'You won't be able to travel as a king. I can get you on as a ship's hand. You will be dressed in worn, torn clothes. You'll help load and off-load the produce at the docks. Charleston first, then Liverpool. When you get to Liverpool, you get on another vessel for Bonny in the same capacity. You will have to become a servant, Jaja. Would you be able to do that?'

The king fell silent.

Cheeks said, 'This is not a lunatic idea, Jaja. It's your only chance of escape. It'll take a couple of weeks to arrange and finalize, so I'll need your answer now.'

The two men continued their leisurely stroll in silence. Jaja's gaze was fixed on the ground.

He said, 'Give me a minute. I will return to you.' He disappeared into the wooded area to go to his shrine, the baobab tree. He took a small bottle of rum from his dashiki, uncapped it and splashed some of the contents onto the massive trunk. Placing his other hand above the wet spot, he lowered his head and began to pray as the rum slid into a throat-like crevice at the base of the trunk to unlock the wisdom of the god. Jaja threw more of the rum onto the tree and began praying fervently again. Back home, he would have intoned to Chukwu with splashes of palm wine and, depending on the severity of the need, he would have sacrificed many chickens. He would have done all this in the shrine room inside his compound, himself his own high priest of the Ikuba oracle, robed in red velvet cloth draped over his left shoulder, seated in the room painted white with kaolin, in a chair whose feet were lodged in human skulls and whose arms were the bones of slain enemies. Now, he stood in silence for another minute or two, listening to the ancestral bird voices for the guidance that he needed. He recapped the bottle and rejoined Cheeks who was calmly leaning against a royal palm.

Jaja said, 'Mek we do it, John. Mek we go.'

Cheeks nodded and said, 'A good decision, if I might say so, Jaja. Stay here and you're a dead man. It's your only chance.'

Jaja looked in the direction of the house, but said nothing. He and John shook hands.

John said, 'Think of what it would mean if you succeed! You and I would both have scored a resounding victory against our common foe. I can never forget what they did to my people.'

He again told the story of how his great-great-great-great grandfather had suffered at the hands of Oliver Cromwell, how his grandfather was hung by the British Government for treason, and his father then sent to Barbados as a child labourer, dying at the age of twenty-six. His mother, just turned twenty-one, was a widow with a two-year-old boy to raise. She was of Irish descent; her people had suffered similarly at the hands of the English.

They returned to the public room where Jaja still had his warri board on the floor. He asked John if he would like to learn warri, and, for the second time that day, Jaja taught the game. Jaja felt their deepening bond.

After dinner, John left at around eight o'clock in his double rig for the one-hour ride to Fontabelle where he lived with his mother.

The sounds of whistling frogs came in through the louvred windows, and Jaja's heart filled with hope. His trust in people felt restored. He had an ally, and he had an intimate companion. That night, he slept dreamlessly with Becka in his arms.

CHAPTER THIRTEEN

Becka stood at the back door, arms akimbo, her face greeting the Saturday morning breezes that ruffled the trees. A thick coralstone wall about five feet high surrounded the yard and ended in alignment with the back of the house. Just yesterday, hearing a cacophony from the geese, she'd gone to see what their commotion was all about, and saw a child's head ducking down behind the wall. She had laughed, knowing that the child would have been standing on the back of another child to call to the geese. There would be several children standing by the wall, anxiously awaiting their turn. She'd shooed the children away and threatened to tell their parents, but her laughter had blended with the yard fowls' crows and cackles.

At the yard pipe, she removed a garment from the cane laundry basket, ran water on it, soaped it down with a chunky piece of blue soap, scrubbed it on the jooking board, and rinsed it. For white garments she applied starch. She put the rinsed items into the large galvanize pan. When the pan topped, she deftly flicked each item out, with the sound of a cracking whip, and hung them on the line that ran diagonally across this section of the yard. This was her Saturday morning ritual. While she always rose with the first cock crow, she would get up a little earlier on Saturdays. As her mother used to tell her and her sister, 'Early bird get de sweetest flower.' She wondered how her mother was keeping; she would visit her on Sunday.

She hummed as she worked, pausing only when her thoughts were deeply engaged. As she whipped out one of Jaja's rinsed dashikis, she wondered what the king's future might be. Would he manage to escape the island? If he did, would he reach back to

Africa from South Carolina? Would he keep his promise to send for her once he reached Opobo? Would her mother revive? Could her sister manage to provide for herself and their mother?

Jaja welcomed John Cheeks around three-thirty. On the First Secretary's recommendation, Governor Sendall had approved the reduction of Jaja's security to one guard – an officer stationed at the top of the back staircase which ran down from the second floor. The officer normally sat in the vertical trellised porch there. The back entrance, leading to dense woods, would have been the most vulnerable spot as regards any attempt to escape. Though he had concluded that Jaja posed no real threat in this regard, the Governor knew that an officer at the back entrance would appease the Crown and remind Jaja of the nature of his confinement. The fact that Judge Hanschell lived at Stratford Lodge, the house to the immediate right of Walmer Cottage, would deter Jaja from any thought of escaping from that side of the residence.

As Jaja sat with Cheeks, he recalled the visit he'd received from Hanchell's niece the very day after he'd arrived at Two Mile Hill. The young girl must have seen him arrive from her side window in the Victoria and in his formal European dress. Later that afternoon, as he and Oko Jumbo walked in the gardens, Jaja had heard an adult female voice calling, 'Maude! Maude! Come back here at once, child! Maude!'

But the girl's head appeared over the fence and she called, 'Sir, are you a Prince? And where have you come from?'

Jaja told her.

'Maude!'

Jaja saw an older woman in long-sleeved, high-necked dress approaching.

'Do not trouble the good gentleman, child. Sir, I assure you of my sincerest apologies for my niece bothering you.'

Jaja smiled. 'It is no bother. I am King Jaja. It is good to meet you, Maude, and…'

'We heard of your arrival. I trust you're settling in nicely… Oh, I beg your pardon. I'm Mrs. Hanschell. My husband is Judge Hanschell.'

Jaja nodded.

'Now, let's say goodbye to Mr. Jaja,' Mrs. Hanschell said, before Maude could ask about the king's dog, which also seemed eager to meet her. Mrs. Hanschell gave the girl the firmest of looks. 'Now, come along, Maude. Come along.'

'Oh! Auntie Jane. What will my friends say when I tell them I've just met an African prince!'

Now he and John talked about local matters, though his mind was often elsewhere, while Becka came back and forth with lemonade and other refreshments.

Jaja said, 'I always urge my children to learn merchant and clerk business and study them up to count well.'

'I am sure they will be all right, Jaja. I'm sure that you've taught them well. You musn't worry.' Cheeks detected that Jaja had retreated into the past again, and was in the mood for staying there. He told Jaja he had a particular interest in hearing about the palm oil trade and Jaja told him about the enormous demand for the product in Britain and Europe. He told him how the trade was organized, and of Britain's attempts to take it over and eliminate the African middlemen. Their goal, Jaja said, was to reach the Niger hinterland, the source of the oil, where British traders would set up their own trading posts, without having to pay him tax or 'comey' money. Greed had made them discontented with buying the oil brought to their ships by his canoes and paying the required levies. They were willing to go to any lengths to take over the trade, including his kidnap and bogus trial.

John nodded as Jaja retold his tale. Jaja liked John for his ability to listen. Talking to him purged a little of his bitterness.

Reaching into his leather bag, John said, 'I brought some preserves for you. My mother makes the most delicious things. These are just samples. Let me know the ones you like, and when the old lady makes more, I'll bring you some.' He laid out pots of guava cheese, guava jelly, crystallized shaddock rind, fudge, punch-de-crème, great cake, pudding, tamarind balls, and tamarinds-in-syrup on the mahogany table.

Jaja's eyes twinkled. 'Thank you, John. You be great friend.' He slipped a seedless tamarind ball into his mouth, sucked a little, his taste-buds assailed by the sugar, spice and black pepper that gave way to the fruit's pungency, chewed cautiously and then swallowed.

He said, 'The aftertaste not so bitter as African kola. But we eat kola in small bites and with strong alligator pepper to ease the bitter taste.'

'Are you saying you like our tamarind better than kola, Jaja?'

'I do not say that, John.'

Laughing, the two men rose and headed toward the gardens. Once there, they immediately turned to the escape plan, although there wasn't much to add. John said he was awaiting results of the job request that had been put in by a fourth party, on Jaja's behalf.

He said, 'Jaja, I must say to you that I cannot in any way be linked to this plan. I must think of my mother, you understand? That is why I've had to use fourth parties. Nothing can be traced back to me. None of the parties at the end of this relay even know that I exist.'

'I understand and am grateful for your help, John.'

Suddenly, Oko Jumbo started barking and moving in the direction of a cluster of royal palms, from which two fowls scampered away into nearby brush. Oko continued his vigorous barking, prompting John to remark, 'Your dog well earns his pay.'

Becka noticed John was leaving much earlier than the previous day.

She said, 'You not staying for dinner, Mistuh Cheeks? I cook a-plenty.'

Jaja laughed and said, 'You are going to miss a very good meal, John.' But John politely declined, indicating he'd promised to eat with his mother that evening. Jaja and Becka stood by the doorway and watched the rig until it disappeared.

When Becka heard the last sound of the wheel, she turned to Jaja and said, 'Ev'ry bush is a man, Jaja. Ev'ry bush is a man.'

CHAPTER FOURTEEN

Becka could hardly believe that only a few weeks had passed since she assumed duties as nurse and housekeeper to Jaja. The intensity of her days and her engagements with the king made it seem so much longer. She was glad for the removal of the officer stationed at the side door and for Mr. Brathwaithe's return to Jordans. She could tell Jaja was too. They had revelled in regaining their privacy. As she heard the swelling staccato of the cocks, she felt like a mother hen about to cuddle her chicks. She snuggled next to Jaja and placed her left arm across his chest. The king awoke with a slow chuckle and his own feathered smile.

'My dove,' he said, his voice deep and earthy.

She wanted to remain with him in their nest, but the day's engagements made an early start necessary. She rose from the bed, stretched and dressed. Yawning, she said, 'I gine fix some bre'kfast.'

'I coming with you! I coming!' Jaja threw the sheet off and scrambled out of bed with exaggerated movements that brought laughter. He made faces like a frog's. Entering his game, she pretended a hasty exit from the room, waggling her behind and swaying her hips from side to side. Glancing back, she saw Jaja approaching, naked save for the cowrie necklace and the broadest of grins. She raced out of the room with her hands over her pelvis, laughing and saying, 'No! No!'

Phillips had the Victoria shining. He had already fed and harnessed the horses when Becka and Jaja came into the yard around six-thirty for the five-hour drive to the tenantry, two miles short of Jordans Plantation house, where her mother lived. Their ability to make this trip was more evidence that the colonial administration deemed Jaja a low risk as regards any attempt at escape. Jaja was sure this decision had been made by the First Secretary, who must be tired of having to take him everywhere. These days, he only travelled with the king on official visits. Now Jaja came back to Becka with stories of how people stared at him, a black man, driving such a carriage alone. Children pranced and chased the vehicle as far as their parents allowed. Sometimes, he stopped the carriage and talked with the people, the faces of children and adults alike beaming with pride that one of their own was riding such a vehicle. Children begged for a ride, however brief, but Jaja told Becka that he could not risk the possibility of an accident. He would be blamed; he was, after all, new to carriage driving and feared he would be unable to concentrate with excited passengers aboard.

The lengths Jaja took to explain this to Becka made her feel that he was concerned that she should not be offended by the way he spoke about her people. This sensitivity was one of the reasons he had won her affection. She had put some of the delicacies John had given Jaja in a straw basket, along with bread, cheese and the lemonade she'd made. When she'd hoisted herself into the carriage, Jaja, perched in the driver's seat, lightly flicked the reins to set off. They'd take a rest and eat in the St. George parish churchyard, not far beyond the midway point between Two Mile Hill and Jordans. Jaja looked thoughtful.

'Wha' you t'inking, Jaja?' she asked.

'Just that I remembering British want tek everything from me. Look around you, me dove. Tell me what you see.'

'Tell you wuh I see? De housing o' de carriage.'

'Housing that cost plenty. Just like cottage they put me in. I only one man and they house me in a two-storey cottage with three bedrooms, three public rooms, and three servants rooms. They give me fashionable carriage for rich English ladies to ride in park. They want tek all my money. All these accommodations cost money. I could see a carriage like this for when I arrive, but buggy and one horse enough for when I here to live.'

'Ask de secretary man if he can exchange it, Jaja. Is you money paying for it. Ask he.'

'I will. I will.'

After about three hours, they pulled into the yard of the St. George Parish Church. Jaja parked in the shade of a large mahogany tree, and they got down from the carriage and walked about to stretch their legs. Becka saw the spellbound look on Jaja's face as he beheld the stained-glass windows at the side of the coral-stone church.

'Magnificent building,' he said. 'The skills of British only match by their cruelty.'

'I christen hey,' Becka said. 'And my mudduh used to get clothes and things for we from hey. Duh got one in St. Barnabas just up de road from you. You should go. De St. Barnabas Anglican Church.'

'I will do that, my dove. Maybe this Sunday,' Jaja said.

Further on, fronds of canes waved in green welcome as Becka and Jaja wound their way slowly along the cart road. Large piles of cane, cut and bundled, awaited the morning's carts, sand-coloured cane-trash surrounding these piles. Soon, they reached the cluster of houses in the tenantry where her mother lived.

Each two-room house of unpainted wood and shingled roof in the tenantry stood on coral-stone rocks like someone ready to sprint to the unpaved track that ran through the centre of the village. The families owned their dwellings but not the land, which was owned by the estate. Houses were made so they could be easily moved, Becka explained. Should the landowner ask the house's owner to leave, which was not uncommon, it was possible to dismantle the house and rebuild it somewhere else. Jaja's eye was caught by the flowering hedges of shrubs that added spots of colour at the front of these homes. In almost all the back-yards, rows of ground produce sprouted in glory. Growing okra, yams, sweet potatoes and other vegetables brought their owners a few shillings a week, and gave them a food supply. Yet if the landowner asked a homeowner to leave, only the house could be taken and all the produce had to be left. Becka told Jaja, too, how the whole area could flood after heavy rains, and sometimes be impassable. It was not uncommon to hear of people drowning. The vestries, controlled by the landowners, paid little attention to providing the chattelled tenantries with adequate roads.

A few people walked behind the carriage as soon as it entered the track. Soon, it seemed the whole village had come out as the sleek black vehicle came to a stop. Patsy had been one of the first to spot the carriage, and she headed the throng with her child in her arms. Some villagers hollered and whistled, others laughed, while some stared with open mouths. All the adults knew who the carriage driver was and why he was in the island and that one of their own had been chosen to attend him.

Becka watched as Jaja disembarked, smiling and waving a hand. Did this barefoot throng remind him of his people in Opobo? She saw him hold out both hands in embrace towards the people, though some sorrow seemed to crinkle his brow.

Inside the chattel's first room, Jaja took in the pots and pans hanging from the walls, the wooden barrels turned upside down and used as seats. A huckster's tray leaned against a wall, scratched and stained. A woman in a worn beige cotton skirt and a navy-blue blouse rose from the coal pot she attended on three soot-stained stones in a corner of the dirt floor. Becka and the young woman hugged and exchanged greetings. Then Becka turned to Jaja and said, 'My sister, Frances.' Jaja nodded and smiled.

'Good-day, Sir,' Frances said, and shook the king's hand.

Jaja said, 'How your mudder?'

'She holding on. She sleeping right now.' Frances looked towards the curtained doorway of the other room. 'I gine wake she in a few minutes when lunch ready.'

Patsy sat down on one of the barrels and began to rock her infant. Becka gestured for Jaja to sit on the other barrel, but he declined and settled on the cloth mat near the little side window. Becka's eyes widened when she saw the ease with which he sat on the mat. He lowered himself in one seamless movement as a dancer might. Patsy saw this too. The two of them looked at each other with questioning looks and then broke into laughter.

Jaja laughed and said, 'Ah-ha. I know what make you women laugh. I have to tell you that in Opobo, I take my cane and my goatskin mat when I visit other chiefs and family. So we same, and when I go back to my place, I take all you with me!' His voice rose on the last phrase, and they all burst out in laughter. Frances looked toward the curtain, put a forefinger to her lips, and softly hissed, 'Shhhhh.' Becka and Patsy put their hands over their mouths to stifle their laughter. Then Becka looked at Patsy, and slapped her knees to indicate that her friend should place her baby boy there. Becka began to cuddle the little one, made baby sounds and gently swayed him. She glanced at Jaja and imagined that his heart, like hers, was bucking with joy.

Becka watched as Frances finished cooking, threw some water on the coals, and pulled back the curtain which divided the two rooms. When she heard her mother's low voice, Becka immediately got up, gave the baby to Patsy, and went to her. Her mother's blood disorder had weakened her and Becka could see she was losing weight rapidly. The vestries, who were charged with providing health care to the very poorest, were too far away in the city for Frances to take her. They wouldn't have helped her mother anyway because she was receiving money from her son in Panama, and Becka now had a steady job. The medicines that Frances administered to her mother were traditional ones, like milkweed to cleanse her blood, and a variety of bush teas to make her sweat, calm her nerves, and help her sleep. Sometimes whole plants with the soil attached to the roots were placed in the mixture.

'How Fred?' Mrs. Jordan asked, as she did daily, of her son, as she sat up painfully in the low wooden bed. Frances replied, as she usually did, that they hadn't heard from him in a while, but that the last time he wrote he sounded all right.

'Yuh know, I does put somet'ing one-side from wuh he does send, so I doan ha' tuh depend on de vestry. Miss Mavis down de road pass 'way last year, causing when she tek-in and report she sickness to the Guardians. By de time it tek fuh de medical officer to see she, and de ticket fuh she medicine get sen' to de dispens'ry at de almshouse, Miss Mavis did in another world...'

Becka felt pained by her mother's slow speech and the weakness of her voice.

She said, 'Doan worry, Ma. I know how um is fo' we poor people. Everyt'ing goin' work out. Rest yuh voice, Ma.'

Returning to the other room, Becka helped Frances serve the cohoblopot of meats and vegetables mixed in with rice. Frances fixed her mother's plate first so that it would not be too hot when she was ready to eat it. After lunch, Becka took Jaja outside and together they watered the horse from a wooden bucket. Afterwards, they sat next to the carriage on Jaja's mat and talked in the mango's shade under which it was parked.

When she re-entered the house, Becka noticed that both Patsy and Frances were giving her the eye. This was something among women, and they could see that Jaja had no idea that they *knew*. Frances had gathered a pile of vegetables in the centre of the floor – mangoes, yams, potatoes, breadfruit – some grown at the back of the lot they rented from Mr. Brathwaite, some from Patsy's. Becka placed them in the flour bag which Frances provided.

'Thank you, Frances and Patsy,' Jaja said, and slightly pursed his lips. Becka saw a gleam in his eyes. He was no doubt recalling his own hospitality rituals. He had described them in such vivid detail to her, the ritual of the kola nut, the alligator pepper, the pots of steaming food and the palm wine to wash it down – each visitor leaving with a bag of produce. She could live in Opobo, in that familiar vein, with the king, but not now, not with her mother still so sick.

CHAPTER FIFTEEN

Next day, the First Secretary's double buggy pulled into the driveway around 10.00 a.m. Jaja was reading a newspaper in one of the public rooms when he heard Becka's call. He rose with his cane, though he rarely used it nowadays, and reaching Becka where she stood by the sink washing wares, he gently squeezed her buttocks.

Becka said, 'Leh me 'lone, Jaja. You too frisky.' But she returned the squeeze on the part of the king's anatomy.

Laughing as he left, Jaja said, 'And you frisky too, me dove. I take you to Opobo when I leave this place.' He kissed her. He and Becka had almost complete privacy. The sole guard on the back porch of the cottage's second floor could neither see them nor hear their conversations. Jaja, however, thought it possible the guard could hear their loud laughter. Sometimes, he and Becka laughed even more loudly so that the guard would wonder what they were doing.

In an hour or so, Jaja reached the city. Before pulling into Queen's College's carriage way, Jaja looked across Constitution Road to the large property on its opposite side. It had a military aura about it. No garrison, no fort or fortress, no soldiers, but a Spartan precision in the neatly trimmed hedges and trees behind the tall iron fence that surrounded it.

'What be that place? Who live there?' he asked.

The First Secretary told him that it was the residence of the officer who commanded the Barbados troops.

'Barbados is Britain's military headquarters in this part of the West Indies,' he said. 'And the British Government is rightly proud of it.'

'I understand.' The military talk made Jaja think yet again of the enormous risk he was taking. He expected John to visit on

Wednesday, in two days, and hoped he would bring more detailed news about the escape plan.

The First Secretary parked the buggy in the shade of a tree that rose from the centre of the school yard, its leaves a fountain of green. A small group of women stood in the wide-columned front porch and looked towards the carriage and at the two men approaching. A fine-featured woman, perhaps in her late twenties, wearing an off-white, ankle-length cotton dress with ruffles at the shoulders and cuffs, stepped forward. With a military precision, she extended her hand to the First Secretary and introduced herself as Miss Helen Veitch Brown. The First Secretary introduced himself and Jaja. Miss Brown nodded toward the king and turned to lead the party into the building.

'How flattering of you to come to see our school,' she said. 'My work here has been nothing but a most pleasant experience, both with my students and my teachers.' She looked towards the other three women who smiled collectively.

'We have a few minutes before the students present their annual cantata. If you gentlemen would care to join me in my office, I can give you a brief history of our school.'

As the three young teachers continued down the corridor, Miss Veitch called after them, 'The stage curtain! Do tell them to fix it properly!'

Inside the office with its large picture of Queen Victoria on the wall behind her desk, Miss Veitch told them how in 1683 Colonel Henry Drax, owner of Drax Hall Plantation, had provided funds in his will for the building of the school. But Drax's dream, she said, because of the most pernicious politics of the time, had not been realized until January 29th 1883, when the school opened with thirty-three female students ranging in ages from three to nineteen. By December that same year, enrolment had risen to sixty. The school offered English, French, Divinity, History, Geography, a branch of science, and class singing. Parents who had a particular desire for other subjects could have those added.

'Miss Germain was to be our very first headmistress. But, poor lady, she died just shortly after arriving here. Consumption, I think. Her constitution couldn't withstand the long sea journey from England. So, sadly, she never commenced her duties here.'

'And how long have you been headmistress, Miss Veitch?' the First Secretary asked.

'Almost eight years now,' the headmistress said with a flourish. 'I came with the winds of '83.' Her theatricality amused Jaja. He had got used to her precise, matter-of-fact speech. Now she was exhibiting a levity which the king found endearing. She must have got used to them and felt more relaxed.

'Your place very pretty and large. You do well here,' Jaja said.

'Thank you. We share this commodious building with Combermere, which is a boys' school, but it is my wish, at some stage, to petition our Board of Governors to look into the possibility of us solely possessing the site. You see, judging from the rapid growth of our enrolments, we will soon need all the space to accommodate our girls.'

The hall had filled by the time Jaja and the First Secretary entered. The audience, made up of students from both Queen's and Combermere, their families, and friends, was humming in anticipation. When the call was made by a tall, brown-haired teacher, everyone rose to sing, 'God Save the Queen'. Then groups of performers, in turn, came onto the stage. Songs in two-part harmony. Songs in three-part harmony. Soaring solos. Jaja recognized the piano accompanist. She was one of the three young teachers who had welcomed them on their arrival.

During the reception which followed the performances, Jaja began to feel a little weak and indicated he wished to leave. Something he'd eaten hadn't agreed with him. So he and the First Secretary said their farewells and appreciations to the headmistress and left for Two Mile Hill.

As they entered the Walmer Cottage yard, Jaja saw Worrell walking away from the side of the house toward the gardens at the back of the property. Their eyes briefly met and, in that fleeting moment, Worrell glowered and Jaja smiled. He and Worrell had never been able to patch-up their confrontation that day when Becka had stopped them from coming to blows. He saw little of Worrell now since the arrival of his own personal servant. Judging from the direction Worrell came, Jaja figured he had come to bring Becka some fresh fish. Despite the rivalry, Jaja credited Worrell with bringing the freshest albacore and marlin fish, which Becka cooked to perfection with her seasonings.

Next day, a public holiday, the First Secretary came to take Jaja to the Garrison Savannah to witness the presentation of new colours to the Second Battalion of the York and Lancaster regiment by H.R.H. the Prince George of Wales. Jaja recognized the road after they passed Government House. It intersected with the one he took to Two Mile Hill on the day of his arrival. He seemed to have been in the island much longer than he actually had been. Perhaps it was because so much had been happening. Love can do such things. Love and memories of a past that mingled with the thoughts of freedom.

The buggy pulled in under an enormous evergreen which, from its size, Jaja concluded had to be well over two hundred years old. Several other buggies were already settled in the tree's sprawling shade, their occupants no doubt already relaxing in the stands. Tens of hundreds of working-class people had gathered to witness the ceremony, and they stood by the white railings, umbrella-less in the scorching sun, looking toward the centre of the field where officials and officers of the regiment were sitting on a large raised platform. The masses were here to see the pomp and spectacle and the presenter of the new regimental colours – the grandson of Queen Victoria.

Even now, more carriages were arriving. The First Secretary said, 'Such a vast crowd is to be expected, of course. This is an unprecedented event in this country. It affords our loyal people an opportunity to see the grandson of Her Majesty.'

Suddenly, as they started to walk away from the carriage, a swarm of men, women, and children surrounded them, shouting, 'King Jaja! King Jaja!' A mischievous youth shouted, 'Wey you Bajan woman?' The young man and his laughing friends were slapping each other's hands and shoulders. Children leapt and hopped like bucking lambs. Men and women waved fervently, vying to get near to the king, to glimpse him up close in the sea admiral's uniform he wore. One of their own. A king. Jaja's heart stirred with love and memories as he waved and smiled at the sea of black faces.

The First Secretary called out, 'Move back now! Let us through!' This parted the wave of curiosity, and soon Jaja and his host were seated in the stands, the official explaining the event and pointing out important people, including Prince George, who was just now arriving.

'That is Admiral General Tongue accompanying his Royal Highness,' the First Secretary said. 'In keeping with custom and the occasion, the Prince is wearing a Navy Commander's uniform with the addition of a ribbon across his left breast.' He reached inside his jacket pocket for a pair of binoculars. He raised them to his eyes and, satisfied, passed them to the king.

The ribbon resembled a crest of some sort, and Jaja recalled the manilla-leaf symbol which he wore on his headdress during traditional ceremonies. The Prince stood erect, his frame short and slender. A light-brown moustache with handles rested on his beard. He assumed his position at the saluting post where the Royal Standard floated like the freedom that was never far from Jaja's thoughts. The chaplain of the forces and a Reverend Darnell, in full canonicals, stood on either side of the Prince. The senior officers were next in line, followed by the York and Lancaster Regiment and the West India Regiment in their respective stations. Each regiment comprised two battalions, Jaja was told, and the York and Lancaster Regiment was the county regiment of Yorkshire-Hallamshire in England. The West India Regiment belonged to the Crown and its members were West Indians of colour. Both regiments were identically dressed in red jackets with lapels to the waist, white waistcoats, breeches and stockings, short black gaiters and black shoes. Gold crests were stitched to the fronts of their black hats.

'I do hope it doesn't rain today. It would be a shame to have such a marvellous display spoilt by the weather,' the First Secretary said, looking up at a dark cloud.

The Lieutenants of the Colour party remained with the Company to the right, which formed the escort, while the new Colours, in their dark casings, moved towards the centre in the charge of the two senior Colour sergeants. To begin the ceremony of trooping the old colours for the last time, the band began to play 'Auld Lang Syne' as the old colours passed slowly from the right to the left, before being moved to the rear. Then the consecration of the new colours began with the hymn, 'Onward Christian Soldiers', sung by the regimental choir accompanied by the band. Prayers followed and then the benediction. The purple-robed chaplain made his way toward His Royal Highness, who received the cased new colours from two officers and presented them again, as the officers knelt, with a few appropriate words. The Colonel of the battalion responded, and then the whole party returned to the saluting post and waited for the march-past. As the troops moved solemnly past, the Prince and the Colonel briefly nodded at each officer. The regiments then lined up in formation again, and a royal salute, with the new scarlet colours lowered, brought the ceremony to a close.

By now Jaja's mood had changed. It seemed as if the whole atmosphere had turned grey, even though the hovering cloud had been dispersed by the sun. The dark cloud had entered him. He ached for Opobo, to be attending his own festivals, his own rituals and ceremonies – like the New Yam festival when, each August, the first of the newly-harvested yams would be offered to the gods and the ancestors, and then distributed to the people, and he, the amanyanabo, would eat the first yam as mediator between the ancestors and the people, between the Atlantic's salt and the rivers' fresh water, between gods and men. Memories came of the festival of the new year, when they spent the last night of the old year out on the rivers warding off evil spirits with their drumming and incantations, then were welcomed back by the new year's light and the procession that started the carnival. He recalled the jubilant dancing and drumming around the town that climaxed at his palace where the Spirit of Opobo danced on his roof, followed by a regatta of magnificent canoes, each chiselled from a single trunk. His mind floated to the islands near Opobo ringed with rotang palms and tall mangroves where he'd be entertained with dances, singing and feasting. His desire for his freedom was a swift-oared canoe inside him.

After the ceremony, invited guests entered the Savannah's reception room where the First Secretary introduced Jaja to Prince George. After formal greetings, the Prince of Wales said to the official, 'I will be going to my warship when the reception's over, and I would be delighted to have you and Jaja join me on board.'

Jaja's reply was quick and sharp. He said, 'No, me boy. Your grandmudder served me a dirty trick that way a'ready. I ain't going on board with you.'

CHAPTER SIXTEEN

The next day, Jaja waited in the meeting room for John to arrive. In a white buba, he felt both relaxed and eager for news from his friend. He sat in a mahogany chair with a caned back and seat, the back shaped like a shield, the front of the seat planed in the curving line of a crown, the bevelled foot knobs creating a paw-like effect – the chair of a warrior with its echo of an animal totem. Albeit in miniature, it made him recall his throne. He'd taken Becka's lunchtime soup and his afternoon nap. All he could do now was wait. He went over to a side table for the recent newspapers. From the time he'd arrived at Walmer's he had found and begun to read some of the books in the glass-doored bookcase, and afternoon paper-reading had become a ritual.

The *Barbados Globe* reported on the visit to Queen's College. After an account of the cantata, the article gave a list of guests that included him and concluded by saying 'The poor king selected a number of girls and demanded that the headmistress send them to his residence so that they could become his wives.' He had come to expect this type of absurd maligning of his character in the local press. How could they believe he was so uneducated in the ways of the West as to behave in such a manner? He'd studied them. He'd feted their traders in the large banquet hall in his palace. He was no stranger to Western ways. Almost as if on their own volition, his hands tore the paper in half and tossed the pieces to the floor.

He picked up the day's *Barbados Herald*, which carried an account of the presentation of new colours. It noted: 'In consequence of the pressing crowds, and the ill-conduct of certain classes, who make it a point to misbehave wherever they are permitted to assemble, we did not care to undertake the unpleasant task of walking around, but a vehicle which was encompassed by members of a certain element of the community, was pointed out as the one that King Jaja occupied. Men, women, boys, and girls were conducting themselves in a most unseemly manner around it. We could hardly imagine that the mere presence of King Jaja would so intensify the fervour of the crowd of lower classes around him…'

While not as pernicious as the *Herald's* article, Jaja was pained by the patronizing tone of the writer – the reprimanding tone of 'ill-conduct', the snide references to 'certain classes', the paternalistic 'wherever they are permitted to assemble'. He had read somewhere that Barbados was called 'Little England'. Its press certainly reflected a penchant for an imperial pettiness.

'How are you today, Jaja?' John said as he entered the room.

'John, my friend. Becka did not say you had come.' Jaja got up and they shook hands.

'I'm like family now,' John said laughing. 'No need for such formality.'

He gave the king a brown bag. Jaja looked inside it and said, 'Thank you very much for the cake and the guava jelly. Your mother is greatest woman in the world. Tell her I thank her.'

They played what was supposed to be a brief game of warri, but it seemed no one could win. They kept chasing each other around the board.

About three-quarters of an hour into the game, John said, 'Let's call it a draw, Jaja.'

'No. I beat you.'

John laughed and said, 'You will, only if I leave that seed in my third house.' And he moved the seed one house up the board and snapped his finger mischievously. Suddenly, as if in panic, Jaja's eyes lifted to the window and he saw the evening light receding. He so loved warri that he could play for hours without any awareness of time passing. But he needed to get news from John, information that could not be given inside the house. Privacy was essential. He sprang from the board, conceded a draw, and said, 'All right, my friend. Mek we go.'

In the wooded area of the garden, Jaja strode with the gait of a much younger man. A fearless glow flared from his eyes as he sat down with John on their accustomed bench. The whistling frogs had begun their music.

John said, 'You're set to leave Tuesday week, Jaja. In twelve days.'

Jaja nodded and clenched both hands. The Imo River, that sprawling fluid animal that bore his puncheons of palm oil to the Nigerian coast, widened inside him. He was bursting with excitement – and with the apprehension of a warrior about to face a giant. 'Thank you, John. You be my good friend.'

'For a moment I had this niggling doubt we could not get it arranged, but everything has worked out just fine.'

'Becka will get me clothes to wear,' Jaja said.

'And an old felt hat. The more worn they are, the better. And you should no longer shave, Jaja. A beard and moustache, however small they might be, can only help to make your disguise more foolproof.'

Jaja was to walk to the bottom of Two Mile Hill where a cabby (summoned from Trafalgar Square by someone whom John didn't know) would pick him up and take him to Roebuck Street. He was grateful that John had been frank with him, letting him know that he had to protect himself from being implicated in any way in the escape plan. Jaja was glad to know that, should anything go wrong, his friend would not be implicated. From Roebuck Street, Jaja would walk to the Wharf and ask for a man named Yearwood.

John reached into his jacket pocket and withdrew a sealed letter. 'As soon as you arrive, find Yearwood and give this to him.' Jaja was then to board a lighter with its sacks of sugar and barrels of rum and molasses en route to a cargo steamer berthed in Carlisle Bay. Some of the cargo would be off-loaded at Charleston, South Carolina; the rest, mostly sugar and rum, at Liverpool, England. Once in Liverpool, he would board another vessel for Nigeria.

By the time they were back in the house, night had fallen. John left straightaway, waving to Jaja as his carriage pulled out along the driveway. As Jaja stood in the middle of the yard watching the carriage leave, he saw Worrell appear at the southeastern corner of the house, coming towards the yard.

'What are you doing here so late?' Jaja asked. Worrell stopped and said nothing, as if trying to decide whether or not to proceed. Suddenly, he turned around and walked briskly in the direction of Two Mile Hill Road.

Jaja shook his head, thinking, 'If he be my servant, I crush him long ago for his insolence.' Then a familiar arm fell like moonlight on his shoulder.

Becka said, 'Ev'ryt'ing good?'

'Yes, me dove, but that man should not be here so late. Worrell no fit touch me. He refuse to answer when I ask what he doing here. In my country, I would not allow such insolence to pass unpunished.'

'And de plans?'

'I leave in twelve days. The twenty-fourth March.'

'Dah is a Tuesday.'

'You get clothes for to dress me and de old hat. I dress like servant so no one recognize.'

'I get dem fo' you,' Becka said, repeatedly patting his shoulder.

As they strolled, arm in arm, toward the side door, Jaja felt freedom sound in his belly. It rose like the rattle of cowrie shells on a dancer's ankles and the swelling boom of the djun djun drum. It filled him until he felt he would burst. It choked him so that words suddenly became inexpressible.

Finally, two words left him. He looked steadily into Becka's brown, almond-shaped eyes and said, 'Me dove.'

CHAPTER SEVENTEEN

Becka left her mid-morning cleaning to answer a knock on the door. Jaja had taken Oko Jumbo for a walk around the grounds. She opened the side door to see Worrell standing there in brown gaberdines and a white cotton shirt rolled high on his upper arms. He appeared uncharacteristically grave. Phillips had gone to town to purchase two bottles of rum for Jaja. In recent days the king had been sprinkling the spirits more liberally on the baobab's trunk, and Becka knew why. He never drank the rum himself ('Drink make man fool,' he'd say) but flung it on the tree to conjure his god. She'd accompanied him on several occasions when he'd grown restless and unable to sleep.

The atmosphere at Walmer Cottage had become calmer since Phillips had come. Now Worrell just maintained the grounds, the yard, and the kitchen gardens, looked after the cow and the horses and bought food supplies at Becka's request. She knew Worrell still had 'hopes', which was why he continued to bring 'a little extra something' when he returned with supplies.

'Worrell, you awright?' she asked. He pressed the worn straw hat more firmly to his head. 'Wha' wrong?'

Worrell said, 'Um is de cow. I t'ink something wrong wid she. She won' eat she food a'tall. None a'tall.'

'Then, you best walk fast and tell Mr. Brathwaite so he can get de animal doctor.'

As Worrell left for Jordans, Becka walked to the shed. The animal lay sleepily on one side with a dour, doe-eyed look. Becka stooped and rubbed her hand slowly over its head and side. Squatting, she continued to comfort the animal for a while before returning to the house.

As she swept the public room, she couldn't stop worrying

about Jaja being caught or killed as he tried to escape. Later, she'd go over to St. Barnabas Church at the top of Two Mile Hill and get the used clothes and hat for him. If her mother recovered, and if Jaja made it back to Nigeria, she wanted to join him. She knew Jaja loved her and that he would make their reunion a happy one. She didn't care that the rumours of her relationship with him had spread throughout the neighbourhood. She was not ashamed; not a single ash-flake of guilt.

Their bond had startled her, like some suddenly recognized truth. Becka saw Opobo as clearly as daylight – the children walking and playing along muddy tracks, just as they did in Jordans tenantry, or in the nearby woods where sunlight peeped between leaves and cast shapes of light and shadow onto the footpaths. She was sure that she would know Africa through the lines of palm-thatched huts and the dirt yard kept immaculately clean; the hand-held pestle grinding pepper in a mortar; the celebratory days when a pig or a sheep was slaughtered and the rum passed around; the days when the tuk drummers invoked the deep husky voice of the past and a living future through their rhythms. Jaja was that African body, which she, like every one of her kin, knew she possessed. Jaja's presence had filled her with a knowledge that was both rational and inarticulate, had given her keener ears and eyes for traces of her past. So, as she finished her cleaning and opened a sash window to let in the minty breeze and sunlight, her body quickened with the sense of being born again.

She knew Jaja was under immense pressure – the fear of being discovered coupled with the excitement of gaining freedom. Over the past few days she had seen signs of both vulnerability and strength in his face, and there had been moments when she wanted to beg him not to proceed with his plans. When she felt like that, he seemed to understand her thoughts and would say in a voice as reassuring as the bellow of a healthy ox, 'Don't worry, me dove. I am a warrior. It be better to die with honour as warrior than to not see my place again.'

The north-easterly breezes blew across the garden bringing the scents of jasmine, mint and parsley floating through the room, comforting as a friendly ghost. Becka raised her head as she inhaled them. She was thankful for Jaja, and she was thankful for the job that not only provided an income but free lodging and meals as well. Her money was helping to keep their mother alive. She again inhaled the mint-tinted air and whispered thanks.

She heard the side door open and knew Jaja had returned. He had recently taken to bringing Oko Jumbo into the house, though Becka had insisted that this only be allowed briefly, as when Jaja sat in the public room to read or relax – and Oko was never to come inside the house unless Jaja brought him. Jaja had obeyed these rules. Oko's alert ears, long forehead, and powerful, muscular legs made him appear as though he was always on guard, always ready to defend. She looked at him for a while, and he looked at her. She would say, 'I badder than you, Skipper', and he always opened his mouth, lolled his tongue and wagged his tail.

Jaja said, 'He like you voice.'

Becka curtsied in jest and stooped to pat Oko's head.

'I gine soon get you some lunch,' Becka said. 'You want anything in particular?'

'Soup be good as usual. I never turn down you soup, me dove.'

As if in sudden recollection, she said, 'Jaja, de cow sick. So I gine ha' to ask Worrell to get you some cow or goat milk from Mr. Inniss down de road 'til she recover, hear?'

'That is good. It happen when?'

'Jus' dis mornin'. You wus out in de garden wid Oko. Worrell gone in de country fuh de doctor. But most likely, he goin' come in de morning.'

'I hope she survive. She serve me well.'

'When you tek you nap, I goin' go up de road by St. Barnabas Church to get de clothes fo' you, hear?'

Jaja nodded and Becka watched as he and Oko slipped into a meeting room.

The soup Becka stirred contained crab meat and cavali fish, split peas, eddoes, sweet potato, yam, cabbage, carrots, and dumplings. It was rich in seasonings like thyme, parsley, basil, and dill. There were two bowls on the tray she brought with her into the meeting room. Oko started acting up at the smell of the food, so Becka took him outside and put him in his kennel. She went into the cowshed and briefly checked on the animal. It was asleep but breathing. She reported this to Jaja as they slowly blew on their spoonfuls and sipped in silence.

Jaja said, 'I dream of Opobo night and day. I send for you when I get back to my place.'

'I hear de trip real long. I worry fo' you, Jaja. Weeks and weeks 'pon de water.'

'Don't worry, me dove. I feel strong enough for long journey. Your god and my god not desert us. If I find myself to lose heart, I think of your sweet face.'

'You and you sweet talk.'

'I mean my word.'

'Since you leaving Tuesday week, I stay here wid you.'

'You no go to see your mudder dis weekend?'

'Yes, I goin' dis weekend but not de next one. De next one would be we last one together, so I would stay here. We could go to St. Barnabus Church service dat Sunday and pray for you to get home safe.'

'That be good,' Jaja said. They finished their meal in silence.

Around one-thirty, Becka left the yard in the direction of Two Mile Hill with a large straw bag. Yellowbreasts, wood doves, blackbirds, and sparrows twittered and darted from tree to tree. On both sides of the pathway, the leaves and the long dark tongues of flamboyants chattered incessantly. Coconut and palm-tree fronds twirled in sensuous slow-motion, like the arms of men and women dancing to a tuk-drum beat. Becka's high-collared, long-sleeved white cotton dress rustled at the hems. In her heart, joy and fear continued to wrestle as she entered the church yard. Several women and a few men stood in two lines leading to a low building. Becka had been for such aid before at the St. George Parish church, and she knew what to do. As she stood with two other women and a middle-aged man in the line to receive clothes, Becka looked across at the much lengthier food line. She was grateful to the church for providing food and clothing to needy members of the community. This was far preferable to going to the Vestry with its intrusive questions, its favouritism toward poor Whites, and interminable delays.

The woman in front of her turned and said, 'Afternoon.'

'Afternoon.'

'You face look familiar. You live round here?'

'I wuk at Walmer Cottage. I do housewuk there.'

'Oh,' the other woman said. 'You is Becka? You is de house-keeper fo' de king from Africa?' She nudged the woman in front her. 'Mabel, dis is Becka, King Jaja housekeeper.'

The middle-aged man had heard the women's exchanges and, as he walked away with a pair of pants and two shirts draped over his arm, he kept looking at Becka. Then he started laughing and shaking his head.

Becka became sharp and defensive. Her ears pricked like Oko's, and she set her two feet apart.

'Doan mind, Browne,' the first woman said. 'Look, Becka, de people 'round here talking 'bout you and de king, but wuh wunna do is wunna business…'

'And wuh it is dat we do? Huh?'

'No, I doan mean it so. I mean…'

'You doan know wuh a housekeeper does do? So tell me wuh you mean. Tell me!'

The woman fell silent, and Becka stood, her arms folded, feet spread apart. She was about to leave the yard, but Jaja's imaginary arm held her back. She'd stay for him. By the time she got served, she'd hardly noticed that there were now several other people in the line behind her.

As she neared the entrance of Walmer Cottage with Jaja's clothing safely stored in her bag, she heard footsteps behind her growing louder and more distinct. She turned around. It was Worrell, breathing heavily and sounding winded.

'Girl, I didn' know you cud walk suh fast.'

'Worrell, you know you frighten me? Wuh you sneak-up on me so fo'? A few minutes earlier and I would o' crush you from ten feet up in de air.'

'Wuh you mean, Becka? Wuh you mean?'

'Nevuh mind. Yuh don' sneak-up 'pon people so. You now getting back from Jordans?'

'Yeah. Dr. Proverbs comin' in de morning. How she is?'

'She sleeping all de time, but she living. I was checking 'pon she all day. I hope she live.'

'I hope so too,' Worrell said as they entered the walkway into Walmer Cottage. Then she felt Worrell's arm around her waist.

'You know how much I like you and want you, Becka. Wuh he got dat I ain' got?'

She pulled his arm away with a stern, 'Worrell!' But he wouldn't stop. He took hold of her again, this time more aggressively, and in one swift manoeuvre pulled her off the path and into the brush that rose between the towering mahoganies and flamboyants. The straw basket fell from her shoulder and lay like a dead animal on the ground. As Worrell pulled her down, the trees' branches reeled above her. On her back she saw the sunlight glistening like knives. Worrell had hoisted up her dress. She noticed the smell of rum as his breathing grew heavier and more erratic.

In desperation she screamed, 'I see Phillips coming! Jaja servant coming! Leh me go! I goin' tell Jaja 'pon you!' This was just enough to momentarily stop Worrell and give her time to wriggle out from under him. She seized her bag and fled to the house. At the side door, she brushed herself off as best as she could, breathing deeply to regain composure. She saw her dress had been torn, one long running gash the length of her right thigh. She would not tell Jaja about this, but as she entered the house, she met the king coming from the kitchen with a glass of water.

'What happen, me dove?'

She fell into the king's arms, but held back her tears. 'I slip and fall down coming in just now. Nuh problem. I awright.' She wouldn't say a word to the king, although she was sure Worrell thought she would. Now she, too, wondered what Jaja had wondered when he'd run into Worrell coming from the grounds the previous night. Why had he been at the house so late in the evening, he who usually left no later than five o'clock?

CHAPTER EIGHTEEN

As soon as she rose next morning, Becka went to check on the cow, still lying down, but still breathing. It was nearly nine o'clock when the veterinarian arrived in his buggy. Becka's face burned with impatience.

Dr. Proverbs leaped from the vehicle with agility and grace. He could have been in his forties but looked a much younger man. He said, 'I came as fast as I could. I couldn't do more than double the speed, you see?' He was wearing a grey suit and tie, white, wide-rimmed, banded straw hat, and carried a black gussetted leather bag. He followed Becka to the pen. She left him there and went to tell Jaja of the vet's arrival. She was about to return when he told her to sit down and eat breakfast with him.

As they ate silently, a human bridge between the past and the future, thankful for life, for this moment together, Becka felt calm return to her, felt herself enveloped in her own warrior-woman mantle. Her mind had locked with his in facing the future with courage.

She recalled her first meeting with the king, how polite he'd been when she'd gone to his room to change his bed linen and properly introduce herself. He'd made her feel so at ease. 'Come in, me girl,' he'd said. Jaja had not closed the door after she entered and, even though she'd sensed his eyes on her, she felt secure. She was no virgin and knew what men wanted. Her fear of molestation had been real, but the king's respectful distance, his politeness and consideration, had allayed those fears, so that not long afterwards, when she felt a desire moving up her thighs, she'd willingly reached out and touched the cowries that gleamed on his smooth skin. These thoughts kindled the now familiar urge, and had it not been for the presence of the veterinary doctor outside, who might at any moment knock on the door, she would have touched those cowries again.

A knock on the door did indeed interrupt her reverie, and she went out to hear the doctor's verdict on the cow. Dr. Proverbs told her that the cow was suffering from a mineral deficiency and, before leaving, he gave Becka a phial of tablets. He told her to give the animal one tablet twice a day and to make regular checks on her over the next few days. He boarded his buggy with the same alacrity with which he'd descended and soon disappeared around the corner of the house.

Back inside, Becka found Jaja in his favourite meeting room reading the newspapers. He looked up, semi-pursed his lips and said, 'Me dove.' He laid the newspaper on the side table to show he was giving her his full attention.

Becka said, 'From de time I see you I did like you, Jaja. Yesterday when I went to get de clothes fo' you I grow to over ten foot in Saint Barnabas churchyard when a foolish woman start talking you name. Since you come, tings happening that only used to happen in dreams.'

'Nnee,' Jaja said, with a puckered smile. Very rarely did he use African words and this was the first time she heard him use this one. He told her it was a greeting of endearment given to a woman, something like "Hello, my love". She knew his height must have grown too, perhaps even more than hers, so he could see Opobo far across the sea. She felt sure he had a profound confidence in his personal god to realize the dream of return. Her faith locked with his.

She said, 'Ev'ryt'ing good, Jaja. Ev'ryt'ing good.'

Her need to spend time with him had grown stronger. In ten days, he would be gone. Until then, she would savour every moment with him. She had memorized the information he'd given her about the voyage home. She'd had no sense of where countries were until the day Jaja showed her a world map with the British Empire marked in pink. Jaja had pointed to the places where he would stop en route to Opobo, and she had absorbed each landmark and the vast waters between them. She would be with him each mile of the journey with her ten-foot heart of love.

Later in the afternoon, as they strolled through the gardens, he curled his right arm across her shoulders and her left arm rested on his waist. Her mind travelled to his mythical Opobo, its footpaths leading to streams where girls and women washed clothes and collected water for cooking, where women and young men entered the forest, returning with firewood to the compound of thatched huts. She heard a tuk drum coming from one of the huts and saw a young woman, with waist-beads and dark stripes painted on her back, dancing in the centre of the compound, cowry and brass anklets rattling in the sparkling language of betrothal. The woman turned and her glistening face and upper arms revealed touches of camwood, and stripes similar to the ones that decorated her back. Sweat gleamed on her bare midriff and ran down into the waistband of her short multicoloured skirt. The dancing woman's face was hers. Then she saw Jaja emerge from the hut with an intricate headdress of manilla leaves shaped like the head of a hawk. He walked towards her, a broad smile on his face. A ceremonial shawl, draped under his left armpit and looped over the top of his right shoulder, reached to his ankles.

Oko's sharp bark brought Becka back to Walmer's woods. She and the king momentarily separated as they turned around to see Oko chasing a lizard and then a low-flying butterfly. Tongue lolling and little pigtail wagging, Oko suddenly stopped by a low bush near a cactus plant and hoisted a hind leg. Becka and Jaja, laughing, resumed their stroll. The king's right arm was a reassuring branch around her shoulder.

CHAPTER NINETEEN

The First Secretary came around at eight-thirty the next day, Saturday, to take Jaja to the Garrison Savannah to watch a game of cricket. The Barbados team would be playing a practice match in preparation for the first West Indian Inter-Colonial Tournament to be held in September at Wanderers Ground, Bay Pasture. Jaja had heard about cricket in conversations with British merchants and traders whom he entertained at his palace, but it wasn't a game that was played in Opobo. Opobians played more cerebral games like warri or, on the other extreme, very aggressive sports such as wrestling. In St. Vincent, he'd been to several cricket games. At first, he'd found cricket too dull, and the men with little schoolboy caps and padded legs running or walking like ladybugs, too silly. It always amused him when he saw the wicketkeeper and fielders around him squatting like men having a bush stop. He'd shaken with laughter to the puzzlement of the St. Vincent official who took him. But in time, Jaja began to appreciate the strategies of the game, such as a captain positioning fielders for the fast or spin bowlers to force certain plays by the batsmen that increased the batsmen's chances of being caught; or the use of the googlie by a bowler which was designed to make the batsman play in the opposite direction to how he thought the approaching ball would turn. In this way, the batsman could be bowled by leaving his wicket unguarded or be struck on the pad and be given out, leg-before-wicket. When he realized how much like warri the game was, the subtle strategies and the cunning that were involved, he'd come to love and respect the game. He had lost interest in all social events in St. Vincent because of his emotional and physical ill-health, but now love, friendship, and the possibility of escape had quickened him and his love of life had returned. He'd risen much earlier than usual, and when he heard the wheels of the carriage, he was already dressed and waiting by the side door so that the Governor's representative wouldn't have to disembark.

The First Secretary also seemed eager to see the match.

'Five months or so from now, we'll be hosting the first Inter-Colonial Cricket Tournament. Imagine that! Since 1865 we've had Inter-Colonial matches; now, come September we'll be inaugurating the first ever tournament. That's going to be something.'

Jaja nodded as the carriage turned right onto Two Mile Hill.

'The earlier matches be popular to be leading to such big tournament?'

'Of that you can be sure. Of course, there weren't many. Just ten of them over the twenty-five years. I wasn't here in those early days, but I was told conditions weren't half as good as they are now. The outfield at the Savannah would be high with grass, and you could not run after a ball. The pitch itself was so studded with small pieces of coral that the ball had to be changed twice in an innings. The mangled balls were brought back as mementos. I was here, however, for the last of the Inter-Colonial matches in the '87-'88 season. Tragically, we lost to British Guiana by a hundred and eight runs and six wickets.' Cricket was clearly in the First Secretary's blood.

The carriage moved at a leisurely speed, passing city-bound hucksters with boxes and bundles of produce. Teenage girls, and occasionally small boys, accompanied some of them, the girls like the women wearing head-ties and carrying bags of produce.

The First Secretary continued, 'But Barbados has the best team, of that you can be sure. We have won more games than any other team. Did you know that the first West Indian team toured North America in '86? First time for our lads to tour abroad. Twelve two-day matches, mostly against club sides. Six in Canada and six in North America. A return tour by the Gentlemen of the USA followed the next year.'

Jaja asked, 'What other teams will play Barbados?'

'The same. British Guiana and Trinidad. Just the three territories for the tournament. And Barbados will win!' The First Secretary rarely laughed. His wit was dry, and any light-heartedness was delivered with a stiff lip. But after predicting the Barbados win, he released a laugh that surprised Jaja. It was the first time he'd ever seen the man's full set of teeth.

He talked cricket nonstop for the two-hour ride to the Garrison Savannah. Jaja didn't mind. That was how he learned, by reading and by listening. A good listener reduced potential threats from the speaker and attentive listening was a form of flattery. Jaja was more than happy to oblige. Although there remained a polite distance between them, Jaja was ready to exploit any chance of good will. This strategy had already worked for him in the slackened security and freedom to take carriage rides on his own.

The match started promptly at eleven o'clock. The players were walking onto the field and taking up positions when Jaja's carriage arrived. The driver stopped under the shady span of a sandbox tree and jumped down to join the dozens of working men leaning on the track's railings. Jaja and the First Secretary remained in the carriage which, parked just yards behind the railings, afforded them quite a good view of the playing field.

Jaja was told that the practice teams comprised players from the Wanderers and Pickwick cricket clubs, the best in the island.

'Who can stop our lads? Look at him bowl!'

Jaja looked towards the towering fast-medium bowler striding up to the wicket.

'He's out! My goodness! My goodness! He's bowled him! Clifford will demolish the Guiana batsmen. Mark my words!'

Jaja saw the bails fly off the stumps like two sparrows. The batsman hadn't stood a chance. The bowler was Clifford Goodman who, with his batsman brother Percy, dominated Barbados cricket.

'Are you enjoying this, Jaja?' The First Secretary seemed taken aback by Jaja's rather less enthusiastic responses.

Jaja *was* enjoying the game, for the same reason as the official – there was plenty of action on the field – but he had long schooled himself to be calm and measured. This was how a king had to be. There were times when you had to do things like order the death of a traitor. He recalled the last such judgment that he had made. He had been in exile in St. Vincent for just a year, when news reached him of his son Saturday's act of betrayal. According to one of his top chiefs, Saturday had been leaking plans of Opobo's resistance to the British consul, and had even sought the help of the consul in acquiring Jaja's property. When Jaja read that Saturday had also taken his favourite wife, Nwaelechi, as his own, he'd written to his senior chiefs, calmly but clinically directing them what to do. He remembered the letter, word for word. *...and if the conduct of Saturday be such as reported to me, and is really true, call him up and take from him everything that he has and lock them up, and do not allow him to go back to his house. Let Chief Shoo Peterside or any other of the chiefs take care of him until, please god, I come back – take all of his wives from him, and all his canoes, and if he should resist and kill anyone, then you must not suffer him to go unpunished simply because he is my son, but you must deal with him according to the law which is life for life.*

The cracking sound of a bat striking a ball to the boundary broke Jaja's reverie. He looked around at his beaming companion. The Crown's official had brought along some sandwiches, glasses, and bottled lemonade for their lunch. As the practice session ended, after they had their lunch, they set off back to Walmer Cottage. All the way back to Two Mile Hill, the First Secretary talked cricket, about the splendour of the Goodman brothers, and about his certainty that Barbados would thump British Guiana later in the year.

It was close to three o'clock when the carriage pulled into the yard. Blackbirds and sparrows chirped and wood doves cooed. Brown, yellow and white butterflies silently fanned the air. Sounds of a distant dog, a crowing cock. The moderate north-east wind urged the mahogany and flamboyant leaves into a steady dance. Once inside, Jaja drank the split-pea vegetable soup Becka had reheated for him. When he'd finished, Becka took him to one of the meeting rooms, and as soon as she closed the door, said in an urgent whisper, 'John did hey 'bout a hour ago.'

'What my good friend want? I no expect him till later evening.'

'He didn' tell me nothing, just that he would come back 'round five o-clock.'

'Maybe he near here and just want say hello.'

'He di' look a lil worried, though. Like he did anxious 'bout something. Like if something unsettle he.'

'You ask him to wait?'

'Yeah. I ask he if he would wait. I tell he you soon get back, but he say he gine come back later.'

'Don't worry, me dove. I go to lie down for a little while.'

'Sure,' Becka said. 'You go an' get you rest.'

Moving slowly up the staircase, a sudden wave of weariness fell on Jaja, a feeling he attributed to the long drive to and from the Savannah. Smiling, he thought about how he'd felt about cricket when he first saw it played in St. Vincent – the "bush-stop" squatting players, the padded "lady-bug" batsmen – and how he'd grown to love the game. He slipped off his snakeskin leather sandals and rolled onto the ancient bed of Opobo, home of peace and home of war, the necessary gateways to ensuring his people's security. He began to feel as though he inhabited all dimensions of time. He thought of the fires that had raged inside his town over thirty years ago, a war ignited by a disagreement between two women at a water well. But peace had been restored after that strife, and he'd established Opobo's importance. It was the new firepower of cannons that had brought him down, brought him here to Barbados. He'd sacrificed his life to save his people by boarding the gunboat bound for Accra. Now he had to return. *Then, in a room in his palace, a female hand would open the special chests that contained the costumes to be worn by chosen women, men, and children. The King of Opobo was coming home. Clothes would be given to the chosen. They would leave the palace and, joined by muscular drummers, would walk to the waterfront to greet their king.*

'John, my good friend. How are you?' Jaja said, as John dismounted from his buggy. They shook hands and John handed over a paper bag that Jaja knew contained cakes and confectioneries.

John said, 'I stopped by earlier. Becka said you went to see cricket. How was the game?'

'I very much enjoy game,' Jaja said. 'Everyone expect you to win big tournament in several months.'

'Who said that?'

'The First Secretary. He be in love with the game. That is all he talk to and from Savannah.' Jaja held up his right hand and moved the forefinger rapidly up and down on his thumb to demonstrate the man's talkativeness.

John laughed. 'Well, I'd have to say on this occasion he is right. Neither Guiana nor Trinidad will be able to stand up to the batting and bowling of the Goodman brothers.'

Jaja turned toward the house but stopped when John did not follow.

'Let's go in the gardens,' John said. 'I can't stay as long as I usually do. I just wanted to update you on things.'

When they were sitting on the coral-stone bench, John said, 'Something has come up. My intelligence indicates we must for a time put things on hold.'

'Why? What happen to bring this?'

'It's just a precaution. There seems to be increased police activity along the Wharf, and I want to be sure it has nothing to do with you. We need to be quite certain of that. Nothing has been called off, you see. As soon as the all-clear is given, I will let you know. I hope by Wednesday. Don't worry, Jaja. There's no need to worry Becka with this.'

The king remained seated, watching John disappear through the foliage leading back to the house. Then he got up and headed for the baobab tree. Once there, he withdrew a libation and watered the throat of the god.

When something suddenly landed on a branch near him, he turned sharply to look around, but when he saw what it was, he relaxed, pursed his lips and smiled. It seemed to him the green monkey's eyes were filled with water.

The god's response and his thoughts about Becka kept Jaja fixed on victory. John's news was a mere delay to the start of the journey that would take him home. He would let nothing stop him.

CHAPTER TWENTY

Becka said, 'My mudder strong. I feel she goin' pull through.' She sat next to Jaja in the sleek Victoria on the way back from Jordans Tenantry to Two Mile Hill. 'Milkweed to cleanse de blood, bush tea to mek she sweat, calm she nerves, help she sleep.' She almost sang this like an incantation tinged with hope and concern.

The sun was setting as they pulled into Walmer's, the carriage wheels settling on the yard turf like a concluding musical phrase, but then the trilling of sparrows, blackbirds and ground doves, the rustling of coconut and palm fronds in the wind's breath, rose and began the symphony again. Becka stepped from the carriage, adjusted her head-tie, and joined the chorus. She was still whistling when she and Jaja entered the house.

'You hand heal me,' Jaja said. 'Healing in you family blood. So you and Frances hand heal you mother too.'

Yet again she was reminded of what had so endeared him to her. He knew just what to say and when to say it. He wrapped her always with a sheltering gaze and softly piercing eyes. She imagined again the docks at Charleston, Liverpool, and Bonny, the king's long journey up the sprawling Imo River and into the creek that took him to his beloved Opobo, the fanfare that would greet him as the boat tied up at the waterfront, the booming drums of his homecoming, the piercing gongs, the rams' horns, the twenty women dancing and singing, their waists and ankles rattling with sound. She saw herself as one of those women, shaking music from her body.

Without changing her clothes, Becka put on an apron, made a tomato gravy, and set it to cook while warming up the okra cou-cou and cavali that Frances had made them. Jaja loved this dish. It reminded him of the foo-foo of home. Becka also made some lettuce juice flavoured with lemon which they sipped with the meal.

'I go to Merchant's Exchange tomorrow,' Jaja said.

'Tell me wuh you want to wear so I can iron it fuh you before we go sleep.'

'Long shirt and gabardine pants good. And my brown felt hat. I hardly wear it since I come and that be true.'

'I go' press de black pants and that nice cream shirt wid de wriggly patterns 'pon it. Wid you brown hat and brown buckle-up shoes, you goin' be dandy.' Becka paused and then asked, 'Evuhthing set fuh Tuesday week?'

Jaja nodded.

'I missin' you bad a'ready. You goin' send fuh me, fuh true?'

'You know that, me dove. You be my wife in Opobo. My family and my chiefs will greet you with great celebration. They present you with gifts of bracelets and beads to wear and shake from you ankles, waist, and wrists. You be my people's new music.'

'And we gine have plenty little Jajas?'

'And a-plenty little Beckas too.'

When she awoke next morning, Jaja wasn't in the house. She knew where he would be, but didn't go to get him. She'd wait for him to return from his sanctuary when he was ready. She opened the side door and picked up the jug of fresh milk that Phillips had collected from a nearby vendor. As she took the milk inside, she thought about the cow in the pen. She had recovered but on the instructions of Doctor Proverbs they were not to milk her until some weeks after the medication had been finished. Even so, Becka crossed the yard and went into the pen. The animal raised its head in anticipation of Becka's hand massaging its smooth black side.

Back in the house, she found Jaja in the meeting room reading a book on West Indian history.

He said, 'What John say about Scottish people be true. It say here Cromwell send them down to this place – some felons, some to pay off bad debt, some rebels like John ancestor. And here I be sent like-a them, away from my people.'

Becka heard his voice falter, went over to him, and rubbed his neck and his shoulders.

'You tell me that. Before I did think all de white people 'bout hey English.'

Jaja said, 'No, me girl. They be Scottish and Irish along with English. The whole place be Great Britain.'

'I doan know how great dum is to treat duh own people so. Nuh wonder duh doan care one flea 'bout we down hey.'

'The same in my place, me dove. The British government come pretending to be our friend, and afterward lying about everything they have written in black and white.'

She patted Jaja on his shoulder and said, 'Leh we continue we talk later. You know you got to eat at a certain time.' She left the king to read and went to prepare breakfast. As she slowly stirred the oatmeal, the old world map he'd shown her hovered in her mind like a magic carpet over the ocean. She'd seen the ships anchored off Carlisle Bay awaiting their cargoes and passengers. One day she'd be one of those passengers making a connection to the land of her ancestors. Charleston. Liverpool. Bonny. The three ports rose in her mind like signposts.

Not long after she'd dried the breakfast dishes, she heard the familiar rattle of the First Secretary's carriage. He had come to take Jaja to see the Merchant's Exchange.

The Exchange was housed in a rectangular building on Pine Street which the driver reached by way of Coleridge Street. He parked in the yard of the three-storey, coral-stone building, which was painted light blue and whose ground-floor doorways pulsed with human traffic. A restaurant operated on the second floor. Its decorative iron-railed verandah featured a shingled roof supported by iron uprights. The top floor had sash windows, the second and ground floors only louvres. Jaja and the First Secretary ascended the wooden staircase to a large inner room on the third floor where several merchants were already seated in low conversation.

A tall man in a tweed suit and waistcoat, with grey side-burns, stood in front of the small group of merchants, poised to read from a document. He apologized for the lateness of the report, cleared his throat and said, 'Correspondence of the Merchants Exchange and News Room, Number Fifty, Pine Street. Advices from Barbados represent the weather as being very favourable, with copious showers of rain. The current cane crop looks ripe and very promising. The manufactured sugar crop for last year exceeded expectations: 45,000 hogsheads of sugar, with 7,593 puncheons, and 800 tons of molasses. Is this report for London approved?'

There were nods from the seated men.

'This document is hereby approved.' Then, before taking his seat, the speaker said, 'It appears we have some guests at the Exchange today.' The First Secretary, who knew some of the members, introduced himself and the king.

The Secretary said, 'It is an honour to have to you here to observe our proceedings. I trust you will stay on for lunch? I don't doubt for a moment you'll find something to your liking in the restaurant below us.'

Another man said, 'The food is excellent. They must have, oh, at least twenty-four different dishes.'

Jaja and the First Secretary listened to the rest of the proceedings, which went on for another hour or so. When the Exchange had ended its business, one of the merchants escorted them to the Reading Room (also known as the News Room), filled with volumes of books, periodicals, and British newspapers.

Jaja asked, 'Do any British papers contain news of my exile?' Before the merchant could reply, Jaja reached into his pocket and withdrew some newspaper articles he had received in St Vincent. 'I present these as gift to you,' he said. The First Secretary seemed surprised by the king's gesture. But Jaja was ready to take any opportunity, however remote, to gain support for his cause.

The merchant went over to a large cabinet where the newspapers were stored and brought Jaja copies of *The Times*, *The Daily Telegraph*, and *Illustrated London News* with strips of white cloth marking specific pages. He directed Jaja to a table where he could sit and read. The merchant and the administrator rejoined the other men in the main room and, about half an hour later, they returned to collect Jaja and take him to lunch.

CHAPTER TWENTY-ONE

The rest of the week passed without a visit from John. What puzzled Jaja was that his friend hadn't kept his Wednesday afternoon visit, hadn't come laden with some of his mother's sweets and puddings. Had the plan been discovered by the authorities? Had John had a change of heart? But Jaja felt too galvanized with hope to let any worry linger. Perhaps John had no confirming news and therefore felt it pointless to visit him. Why would he travel all that distance to say he had nothing to say? This thought kept him confident that all was well. He still felt light as a leaf when the First Secretary arrived early on Saturday morning to take him to visit Glendairy Prison.

They passed through a iron gate set in a wide, thick and very high coral-stone wall, capped with barbed wire, that encircled the compound. The chief warden met them at the front steps of the prison's yellow-painted administrative building.

The First Secretary said, 'Jaja, meet warden, Mr. Senhouse.'

Jaja reached out his right hand which the warden pretended not to see.

'I cannot allow him entry,' Senhouse said, staring straight at the official, with his chin raised.

'He is King Jaja...'

'I *know* who he is. I *do* read the papers.'

'In spite of his circumstances, Warden Senhouse, the Crown has determined he has certain social rights accorded to his station as a king.' The First Secretary's tone was more formal than Jaja had heard before.

The warden said nothing, but his stare indicated disgust.

Jaja said, 'You are a disgrace to your position, Warden. I will report you to the Governor, who will have your rank reduced.'

For a moment, the warden appeared confused, but then he glared at the king.

Jaja turned to the First Secretary and said, 'This man is ignorant. I have nothing to do with ignorant men. Mek we go.'

An hour or so after returning to Walmer Cottage, Jaja was awakened from his nap by the sound of urgent footsteps rising on the wooden staircase. The bedroom door flew open, and Becka burst inside like a powerful gust of wind.

'John hey!'

Jaja rose from the bed, slipped on his sandals, and went downstairs.

As he and John entered the gardens, John said, 'Everything has been cleared, Jaja. Everything's set. You're to go on Tuesday as planned. I came as soon as I could.'

Jaja tossed back his head and looked up at the patches of sky between the silk cotton, mahogany, and flamboyant trees. Then he looked to the ground, to a small area of coral-stone made smooth by the water that cascaded over it during heavy rainfall.

'Thank you, my friend. I be indebted to you. You honour me.'

'Think nothing of it,' John said. 'We're doing this for both your people and mine.'

Back in the house, they played two games of warri; it felt fitting to Jaja that each of them won a game.

Next day, as he dressed to go to Sunday service at St. Barnabas Church with Becka, he looked out of the window towards the kingly baobab tree. The crowing cocks took his thoughts to Opobo and the way the Christian churches and their converts had undermined his people's culture. But he would go with Becka to the church to please her.

Halfway down the stairs, he saw her appear at the bottom. She stood there waiting for him in white shoes and a cream long-sleeved dress. As he drew nearer, he saw she was wearing some of the gold bangles and the gold necklace he'd given her. A hat sat smartly angled on her head and she carried a cream pocketbook.

Jaja smiled and said, 'Me dove. Me beautiful dove.'

'You look real good too, Jaja.' Becka said. 'I going ha' tuh keep all de church ladies from off o' you.'

The steady breezes had moderated the heat so they decided to walk up to St. Barnabas rather than take the carriage. As they strolled along the driveway, they heard a voice calling from the fence between Walmer Cottage and Stratford Lodge, the Hanschells' residence.

'Good morning,' Maude shouted and beckoned them to meet her by the fence. 'Are you going to St. Barnabas Church?'

Becka answered affirmatively.

'Well, my auntie, uncle, and I are on our way. We would be pleased if you would ride with us.'

Becka looked at Jaja who nodded and smiled.

'Lovely!' Maude exclaimed. 'We will meet you in front of your entrance, then.' And off she flew.

The Hanschells also owned a Victoria carriage, a larger and more recent model than the one Jaja used. This was their first meeting with Mr. Hanschell, a burly man in a dark suit and waistcoat, who was highly involved in the commercial and political life of the island, who never seemed to be at home. His round, open face made him look approachable. As the carriage pulled into the St. Barnabas yard, Jaja remarked on the church's fine architecture. He was particularly interested in the bell hanging near the top of the turreted belfry. Underneath that was the arched porch where the last few feet of the bell's rope dangled. The stained glass windows were all similarly arched in shape.

Jaja said, 'Our town bell was erected in 1876. It is not part of any building but stand on its own. Your bell rouse my memory.'

The carriage stopped near a silk cotton tree. The judge stepped down and helped his wife and Maude from the vehicle. After Jaja and Becka disembarked, Hanschell asked, 'And for what purpose do you use your bell, Jaja?'

'To call town together for important announcements; and to alert town of any danger.'

'I see. Ours was erected in 1838, when the church was built.'

Maude was staring at Jaja with a look that suggested (now that she had got closer to him) that she no longer saw him as a prince but as the father of a prince.

The group walked down the red carpet that ran like an artery down the main aisle of the church. Jaja felt Becka's hand clasp his arm. It was a sudden restraining clasp. The Hanschells advanced toward the pews at the front of the church. Jaja looked questioningly at Becka whose hand remained firmly on his arm. She guided him into one of the rows somewhere between the centre and the back. Jaja finally understood and glared like a wolf.

Becka said, 'If black bird fly wid pigeon 'e will get shoot.'

Next day, Jaja read the *Barbados Globe's* report on his visit to the Exchange. It said, 'King Jaja visited the Merchant's Exchange last week and was received with honour by the Merchants. He subsequently visited the Reading Room and enlisted the good offices of a gentleman present therein to read to him paragraphs from English papers referring to his exile. He presented some letters of his own (written to the English Ministers) to the gentleman, in gratitude to the kindness done him. We are glad to say the poor old king is not worried so much now by the idlers in Bridgetown when he makes his appearance in our streets.'

Jaja grimaced. Surely, if he could write 'letters of his own to the English ministers', he was also capable of reading. As for the 'idlers in Bridgetown', Jaja never regarded the ordinary citizens of Barbados in this light. These were his people. Having to wear a social mask when he attended public events was tiring; it was with ordinary Barbadians that he'd felt most comfortable. Yet, if he was to see Opobo again, he knew he must not raise any concerns about his intentions with those with power and connections – and that meant the Whites. He would therefore continue to exercise restraint.

He didn't bother mentioning the article to Becka. There was no need to spoil the positive mood which, from the moment John had given the all-clear, had enveloped both of them. They spent the evening playing warri, strolling in the garden, in each other's arms.

CHAPTER TWENTY-TWO

Jaja had asked Becka to come for him if he wasn't downstairs by five-thirty. Her summons had not been necessary. At five o'clock, Jaja was already outside, heading towards Walmer's woods. He reached his baobab, took the bottle from a pocket of his tattered trousers, uncapped it, and threw some rum on to the trunk. He placed his left forearm on the tree and prayed to his ancestors and to his god for a safe passage. When he returned to the house Becka was preparing a breakfast of oatmeal, bread, eggs, honey and warm milk. She looked him over, pulling his shirtsleeves here, adjusting his hat there. His beard had grown more than he'd expected. The growth, along with the worn felt hat and patched clothes should guarantee anonymity.

After they'd eaten, Jaja was ready to go. At six o'clock, he rose from the table and he and Becka stood in a long embrace near the side door. He'd taken nothing for the journey save his cowry necklace, which he never took off; he had left all his other possessions – his robes and other garments, animal-hide sandals and iron-wood walking canes, and all his jewellery – with Becka.

Jaja said, 'I will miss you, me dove. I will send for you.'

Becka squeezed him tighter. 'Go 'long, Jaja. My god and your god be wid you.'

The cabby was waiting under a flamboyant tree when Jaja reached the bottom of Two Mile Hill about half an hour later. Around seven-thirty, the vehicle was at Roebuck Street as planned. When he reached the Wharf, already alive with commerce, he asked for the man named Yearwood. When a pudgy man with thinning brown hair arrived, Jaja gave him the envelope from John. The man read the contents, took out a pencil, and wrote a note on the letter. He put the letter back into the envelope, handed it to Jaja and escorted him to the waterfront. Yearwood pointed to a lighter that was tied to the moorings and from whose hold rose sacks of sugar and barrels of rum and molasses. Two men were already on the boat; it appeared they were waiting for him and no sooner had Jaja boarded than they rose to standing positions, one at the prow and one at the stern. Each man took up his giant oar and moved the lighter slowly out of the wharf and towards Carlisle Bay.

Near the wharf, the water was dark and turgid, but it wasn't long before sunlight played on the blue of the bay and the steamer came into view. It lay on the water like a long, single-funnelled dash. Jaja had travelled by steamboat before, and he looked to see the vessel's side-wheel paddle and passengers milling on the higher front and lower rear decks. From each deck sprang a masthead from which the British flag flapped urgently. He'd been sent into exile on a steamship like this and it felt fitting that he should escape on one. He recalled the enormous boilers that took up over a third of the ship's interior, the clockwork precision of the hydraulic engine, and the thunderous immensity of the noise that came from it. It would take nearly six weeks for the three-stage journey via Charleston and Liverpool to reach Opobo.

Just a hundred yards or so from the ship, Jaja looked around to take in the coastal view of the place that had been home for nearly three months. The deep green stands of trees, soaring pelicans, and shingled white, yellow, and brown buildings were a backdrop to the oily dark water with its occasional aquamarine highlights. He'd fallen in love with the island's topography, its flora and fauna, and with the winds that were neither too warm nor too cool. All this had lifted his spirits. His love for the physical properties of this place would be forever linked to his love for a woman of the island. As he took in the coastline, he noticed two smaller boats advancing toward the lighter and thought they must be bringing more cargo to the steamer. But when the boats came closer, Jaja could see no cargo on them. Each carried two men facing one another, each manoeuvring an oar. They were white men wearing banded white straw-hats, white long-sleeved shirts, and neckerchiefs. As the first of the boats came up alongside the lighter, Jaja saw navy-blue serge pants that looked official, then the letters stitched on the hatbands that read HARBOUR POLICE. He shrank back from the sudden implication of what he saw. It was as if he had been struck in the stomach by a cricket ball; his breath sputtered like a dying flame.

One of the officers stood up and called, 'We know who you are, Jaja. You are under arrest.'

Jaja turned and dove into the sea. An officer leapt in and caught him seconds after his head went under. He wrestled Jaja to the side of the boat and pushed him up while the other officer pulled the king onto the vessel. The sea water rushed off of him in a gush. The officers held him down until they caught their breaths and then guided him to sit on a cross-plank. Jaja sat unblinking between the two policemen, his body shivering. The other harbour police boat accompanied them back to the wharf.

Jaja looked back towards the open sea as his hopes of freedom receded. He wished he had access to the store of Calabar beans he kept in a secret place in his palace, wished he could grind some of the chocolate-brown seeds, mix them with water and eat them, to end the death his life in that moment had become.

The harbour police held him in a warehouse until the First Secretary arrived. Jaja, head bent, hearing steps sound across the wooden floor, glanced up to see the official's black boots, normally in perfect shine, now covered with a film of warehouse dust. The First Secretary gestured to the two harbour policemen to leave the room, and then he resumed a ponderous, measured pacing across the floor, twice removing and replacing his banded felt hat. He suddenly stopped and said:

'You have let me down, Jaja. I am very disappointed. I have treated you with the utmost respect, tried to make you as comfortable as possible… I could lose my job as a result of what has happened here today.'

'And I have lost my kingdom,' Jaja replied, without moving, though he felt a little regret, too, for this stiff, reserved man he had come to respect. There was nothing else to say.

They drove in silence to Walmer Cottage, arriving there after one o'clock. The first thing Jaja noticed as the carriage pulled into the yard was that a guard had been re-stationed by the side door. Then he heard a loud wailing as Becka suddenly burst past the startled guard and ran towards the carriage. She carried a shawl in one hand and one of Jaja's canes in the other. Her face looked contorted, and as she ran her upper body twisted and jerked in grief.

CHAPTER TWENTY-THREE

Becka looked at Jaja, saw his eyes still had their fierce determination, but that his shoulders drooped. He sat in his favourite caned chair in one of the meeting rooms. Becka felt powerless. What could she do to help him?

The First Secretary, who was standing near the doorway, drew near to Jaja and said, 'I beseech you, Jaja, with Becka in our presence... Who put you up to this?'

Jaja remained silent, stolid.

'You wouldn't like it if the police were to interrogate you. I could have allowed them to do so at the Wharf. Do you know you could be hanged for this?'

Becka folded her arms and sobbed. She went over to the king and placed her hand on his arm.

The First Secretary continued, 'If only you had used one smidgin of good sense, Jaja, you would have abandoned the whole lunatic idea. Look where it has got you. You had under two years left...' The First Secretary's tone wavered between anger and disappointment. When he spoke again, his voice revealed he already knew what Jaja's response would be. 'Who helped you, Jaja?'

Becka watched through teary eyes as the First Secretary turned and left the room. She followed him to the doorway, and when she heard the first turn of the carriage wheels, she returned to find Jaja slouched over on one side, unmoving, eyes shut. She placed her cheek against his face and felt his breath. He looked to her like the tiredest person in the whole world. She helped him up and led him to her room. She laid him on the cot, removed his sandals, and straightened his feet.

Becka tried to be strong, but she felt crushed. All her dreams had shattered like glass. He would be hung. Should she tell the official who was behind Jaja's planned escape? Would this save his life? Or would it get all of them hung? Her instincts told her the latter was the more probable outcome. Who had revealed the plan? It suddenly struck her that she hadn't seen Worrell for days. Did he have anything to do with it? Where was he? Had he stopped coming to work out of shame for attacking her? Or did he not come by the house simply because fish, plentiful from December to April, were scarce as the season neared its end? Phillips was around a lot as Jaja's full-time helper, so she hadn't missed Worrell's help. But could he have had anything to do with Jaja's capture? Had he done this because he knew he had no chance of winning her affections through his senseless attack?

This was the first day Jaja didn't have his afternoon soup. Becka had looked in her room to find him sleeping deeply. Around four o'clock, just before starting to prepare the evening meal, Becka thought she heard a noise in her room and went to check on it. Jaja was groaning and writhing on the bed.

'Jaja! Wha' wrong!' Becka ran to sit on the side of the cot. The sheets were soaked with his perspiration.

He stared at her and, with great labour, just managed to say, 'I... cold.' But when she put the back of her hand on his forehead, she quickly pulled it away. He was burning hot. She turned and fled outside where she found Phillips in the carriage house polishing the vehicle.

'Go and get de Gov-ment man! Jaja sick bad! Tell he is a 'mergency!' Phillips knew he would have to run to Government House, but he did not hesitate. Becka realized that dinner would remain uncooked that evening, but she brewed some bush tea which she made Jaja sip. She stayed up all night helping him to sip the tea and mopping him with towels which she had to wring out in a bucket. By morning, he was no better. Coughing had yielded blood, and a greenish-yellowish mucus joined the high fever and chills. Then he vomited. When she tried to help him up to go to the toilet, he was so unsteady he almost fell to the floor. She barely managed to get him back to the cot. He slowly shook his head from side to side when Becka asked him if he wanted anything to eat. He just wanted to lie down. Becka could only wait for help to arrive.

The crowing of cocks announced the arrival of an enclosed carriage and pair, from which three men disembarked. Becka was already at the door when the vehicle came into the yard. She recognized none of the men, but their white jackets and large dark leather bags indicated who they were. They moved with purposeful strides as Becka stepped aside to let them in. One of the doctors introduced himself as Doctor Archer and presented the others as Doctors Hutson and Bowen. On the way to her room, she told them of the king's symptoms. She left the room, brought in the canister of milk that sat like a lonely castaway outside the side door, and, ravenous because she had not eaten anything for a day, made some breakfast. She took her tray of milk, scrambled eggs, bread, marmalade and tea, to the dinner table and sat there eating, lost in thought. Could Jaja really be hanged? They might just add years to his exile. He would not be able to bear that. All their dreams were slipping away like streams of sand.

What had gone wrong? Who had betrayed Jaja? Had John turned against him? Becka trusted no white man. Had Worrell overheard John and Jaja out in the garden where every bush had ears? Did that explain why Worrell was nowhere to be found? He'd never liked Jaja from the day they'd first met. But what did her thoughts matter, anyway? She had no way speaking to the people in authority, she, a mere servant. All she would achieve if she spoke out would be to invite further punishments, further scrutiny that might very well implicate herself as well. Everyone knew of her relationship with the king. Perhaps, even now, they were thinking that she was an accomplice. Would John say as much if she were to accuse him? Who would they believe? A white accounts clerk? A black maid? She would keep her mouth shut. She wouldn't point a finger.

After breakfast, Becka returned to the meeting room. As she wearily leaned back in his favourite cane, shield-shaped chair, she felt closer to Jaja. This gave her an uplift, a spark of hope in the shadow of death.

Outside, Phillips was still doing his yard work. He brought in some lettuce from the vegetable garden and some golden apples, soursops, and bananas. He told her how pleased he was with the long, wire-hooked stick he'd made to collect the golden apples from the tree. All was normal. Nothing was normal. What had happened to her? She was not the same woman of a few months ago. She felt irretrievably lost, seized by sorrow.

Dr. Archer still carried his stethoscope around his neck when he entered the meeting room. The other doctors gathered around him in a collective jacket of concern.

Archer said, 'It doesn't look good. There is a recurrence of severe bronchial infection and pneumonia, which is why he was sent to Barbados in the first place. But, more than that, his heartbeat is very weak. We have taken a urine sample and will let the Governor know what it reveals. In any event, we'll be back tomorrow with medication. His condition requires immediate treatment.'

'T'anks fo' tekking care o' he,' Becka said, as the doctors turned to go. 'T'ank yuh.'

At the door, Dr. Archer said, 'Make sure he eats something: porridge, soup, fruit. Make sure he gets lots of fluids.' Becka nodded as the men walked toward the carriage.

As the doctors began boarding their vehicle, another familiar carriage crept into the yard and stopped beside it. The First Secretary disembarked, nodded toward Becka who was still standing by the side door, and went over to talk with the doctors. When the doctors' vehicle left, the official passed the guard and entered the house. Becka observed his troubled manner, like someone searching for the right words to say.

'Do you have anything to tell me before I go in to see him, Becka?'

'No, Sir.'

'It is common knowledge that you have a friendship with Jaja. Did he tell you anything? Did he tell you who helped him hatch this lunatic plot?'

'He ain' tell me nuthin', Sir.'

'I find that hard to believe, Becka.' The First Secretary, un-blinking, pierced her with his steady blue eyes. 'Why are you protecting him? Do you know he has over fifteen wives waiting for him in Africa? What place would there be for you if he is ever allowed to return?'

Becka saw through the ploy and repeated, 'Sir, he ain' tell me a thing. For truth.'

Then she asked, 'Tell me, Sir. Duh gine send he back or duh gine kill he?'

'That I cannot say. What Doctor Archer just told me is not in the least bit encouraging. The Crown may not have to punish him if his health doesn't improve.'

Becka could not hold back the tears. Fitfully sobbing, she braced her stomach with one arm and, with the other, pointed in the direction of the room where Jaja lay. Then, suddenly envisioning him being toughly questioned, she put on her shawl of protection and followed him. She knew she could not stop the interrogation, but she would feel better just by being there, and maybe her tears would temper any inclination towards aggression. Thankfully, Jaja was deep in sleep, so she watched the First Secretary turn around and leave the house.

Next day, the doctors returned around nine in the morning. Earlier, she had gotten Jaja some porridge and hot balsam herb tea, which he managed to keep down. She'd also stirred some ground wild purslane (which local people called pussley) into the porridge to help with the swelling of his knees, which had reappeared. When she was ready to sponge-bathe him, she called Phillips to help her turn him over and get him into some fresh clothes.

During the lengthy time the doctors spent with Jaja, Becka cleaned and dusted the meeting rooms and made a fresh pot of balsam tea. This tea had temporarily calmed Jaja's coughing. Around noon, Dr. Archer and his colleagues finally came out of the room and accompanied Becka into the first meeting room.

Dr. Archer cleared his throat and began to speak. Becka did not understand much of what he said. He talked about Jaja's heartbeat being feeble, except for an 'accented aortic sound' and spoke about the visible pulsing of blood vessels at the back of his neck. Archer said there was a slight dullness on the right side of Jaja's lungs caused by 'chronic inflammatory disease' and that his urine was 'pale, slightly turbid, and very albuminous'. Why was the doctor giving her all this complicated information? Granted, she was Jaja's nurse but they knew she wasn't schooled in all the medical big-words. She sensed something that lay just beneath the surface of his words – the reason why Dr. Archer was releasing all this information to her. It was a cry, a personal cry, a confession that he was powerless to help Jaja and this pained him. Most of the people with whom Jaja had any dealings – both working-class Barbadians and members of the Government – invariably became drawn to him. It was his aura of calm, his charm and humour – the same qualities that had attracted the British traders in Nigeria, and had helped him become the dominant economic force in the region. It was clear to Becka that Dr. Archer was moved by the king's suffering.

He said, "Jaja's condition is critical. His life cannot under any circumstance be a long one and his deep depression, no doubt caused by his detention here, is likely to shorten it even more.'

'Wuh cause de feeble heartbeat?' Becka asked.

'Pneumonia and the acute fevers that followed it. He also has developed intestine and liver problems.'

'And you suh somethin' 'bout he blood vessels?'

'Yes. They have started to pulse, almost imperceptibly, but it's there nonetheless. This is due to the walls of an artery weakening.' Dr. Archer opened his black leather bag and withdrew two bottles, a set of syringes, and a sterilization kit.

He said, 'This first medicine is ammoniated tincture of valerian. Give him thirty to sixty drops per day in his tea.' He placed the bottle on the side table. With his eyes on the second bottle, he said, 'This one is strychnia, and he is to be given a sixtieth to a thirtieth of a grain hypodermically (with this syringe) in a little sweetened water.' Using Dr. Bowen's arm for a model, Dr. Archer demonstrated to Becka how to measure and administer the medicine with the syringe and cautioned her not to exceed the dose. When he finished, Becka assured him that she understood the procedures. He closed the bag and said, 'Keep him on a dry diet for a while, anything like cactus, to help him secure a good blood supply.'

CHAPTER TWENTY-FOUR

Over the next week Becka continued to care for the king. On the morning of Saturday, April 4, she went to the bathroom and saw that her rag was still bloodless. Missing her monthly twice in a row had never happened before. Maybe it was the upsets of the last few weeks that stopped the flow. That was possible. She would keep watch. Next month she would know for sure. After her bath, she checked in on Jaja, who was still sleeping. She smiled to herself; the clammy-cherry leaf tea had done its job. If that hadn't worked, she'd have made him another tea of boiled almond leaves. On her way to the side door to collect the milk, she couldn't help but think the darkest thoughts. If he had not already done so, Dr. Archer was likely to give Jaja's health report to the government sometime the following week. What would it mean? Would he be safe from hanging because he was so ill? Would he still be hung in spite of that? Death both ways. Wha' loss!

Each hour, she took a break from the dusting, boiling of water, preparing bush teas, washing clothes, and sweeping, to check on Jaja. When she found him awake, she got him to eat some fruit, or little pieces of cactus or drink the bush tea to which she added the drops of valerian. She had memorized the names of the medicines, "tincture of valerian" and "strychnia", just as she had memorized the ports where Jaja would have docked on his way to Opobo: Charleston, Liverpool, Bonny. Those harbours seemed so hopelessly distant now.

A sudden weariness, a physical heaviness overwhelmed her. She struggled to walk over to the kitchen table where she poured a glass of cold water from the monkey jar. She sat down in Jaja's favourite cane chair in the meeting room. After a while, she reached for one of the newspapers lying on the side table – a

Barbados Globe. She read very slowly, but had become more proficient over the past two months as a result of more regular reading. Her eyes landed on a Trafalgar House advertisement. This was the retailer and wholesaler from which Mr. Brathwaite ordered bulk supplies for both his plantation house and Walmer's Cottage. The advertisement announced the arrival of various goods from London, Liverpool and New York: cases of condensed milk, Robinson's patent barley, Fry's cocoa and chocolate sticks, bags of sago and tapioca, pudding raisins, apples and pears, almonds, and so on. She remembered the first delivery of such goods at Walmer's soon after Jaja had arrived – Worrell cutting the seals and carrying the heavier boxes into the house, she bringing the lighter ones. Such happiness as mistress of Walmer Cottage. The thrill of working near the city. The honour of caring for a king… For a moment she forgot her distress.

Some hours later, Becka jumped up from the chair in which she had fallen asleep. The paper fell to the floor. The house was dark. Through the window she saw the silhouette of trees behind which the moon had disappeared. She found matches and returned to her room to light the candles. Jaja was sound asleep, so she returned to the kitchen to prepare some vegetable soup.

The next two weeks crept by as slowly as a weed-clogged river. Jaja slept most of the time under the various medications. Early one Thursday morning, the team of doctors arrived, and they were accompanied by the First Secretary. Their report was not encouraging. Jaja's condition had not improved. The presence of the official indicated they had expected this. Dr. Archer said the pulsing of the blood vessels at the back of Jaja's neck had become more pronounced and had swollen to the extent that when he listened on his stethoscope, he could hear a blowing murmur.

'It's not just that. Jaja's gait is extremely shaky and weak. It is evident that he is taking very little food and his depression has worsened. Further, his heart, lungs and kidneys are all diseased.' Looking intently at the First Secretary, the doctor said, 'I fear if he is detained much longer here, the result will be fatal.'

The doctors saw themselves out and the First Secretary turned to Becka.

'It is expected he will be sent home. We have already taken measures…'

'Wuh measures?'

'We have telegraphed the Colonial Office to arrange his repatriation, his return to Opobo. Is he awake? There is something I have to tell him.'

Jaja was awake, and the First Secretary told him he was going to be sent home. Becka saw a light faintly flicker in the king's eyes. The official said, 'There is only one requirement, Jaja. I must have your written pledge that once back in Opobo you will not impede our Queen's wish to develop your region. Do you swear to that, Jaja?'

The king slowly nodded. The First Secretary was not satisfied. 'Can you be verbally affirmative, Jaja?'

'Yes.'

When the First Secretary left, Becka ran back into the room. She was happy to know that Jaja, despite his ill health, still possessed his cunning. The official thought he had sworn to abide by the imperial request not to resist British dominance in Opobo. But Becka knew the king's 'yes' meant only that he was physically able to answer the First Secretary's question. She saw the king smile, albeit wanly.

When, a week-and-a-half later, she missed her monthly for the third time, there was more reason for her and Jaja to smile. But this jubilation was tinged with sorrow: Jaja would not see the birth of the child and might never see the child at all. During these days, she'd sit on the side of the cot and hoist her blouse or dress so Jaja could touch her belly. Would he still be there when the baby began to move? If the little one were male she would name him Henry Jaja Jordan. If female, she would name her Grace Sarah Jordan.

CHAPTER TWENTY-FIVE

When the Administrator told Jaja he would be leaving Barbados on Monday, May 11, the king felt something like a warm breeze waft inside him. The thought of one day reuniting with Becka and their child in his palm-rich Opobo brightened his spirits as the steamer *H.M.S. Comus* propelled out of Carlisle Bay. He turned on the bed to face the far side of the cabin and saw his faithful Oko Jumbo curled in sleep. He dreamed to see his place, see his people's faces, drink palm wine from an intricately carved gourd, eat bitter nut, kola nut and alligator pepper, laugh and talk in a circle of family and friends, feel his feet on the clay yard of his compound, hear the laughter of children at play echoing between the huts, their little feet slapping as they ran about, like a drummer's hands lightly tapping out a rapid rhythm near the rim of a *djun djun*.

With Becka's help, Jaja had written a precautionary letter to his chiefs just a week or so prior to his departure. He urged them to be discreet in their actions and not to do anything, however insignificant it might appear, that might jeopardize his return. The British had broken their promises so many times before. Until he set foot on Opobo's soil, he would not lessen his mistrust.

He wrote, 'Do not change any new place of residence, please God, because the British Government will say that it is I who gave instruction to do so. I know them well. They will use this against me. Then they will not let me return to Opobo.' He was confident that the chiefs would heed his words. Now, he fixed his thoughts on the voyage. In two weeks or so he'd touch the coastline of his beloved country.

As the days at sea passed in their almost seamless way, Jaja occupied his time reading his natural history books. In time, he regained enough strength to take very brief walks about his cabin. These walks were slow and painful, but Oko Jumbo happily wagged his tail as if to encourage him. Jaja's cabin was located close to the front of the ship, as far away from the engine room as possible. Sometimes, the king would pause by a porthole and look out onto the heaving Atlantic from which occasionally the leaping arc of dolphins punctured the coal-dark water. But he could stand for only a few moments and would soon limp back to his bed.

One night, as the vessel moved on its eternity of water and darkness, the king's dreams and memories wrapped themselves in ceremonial cloth and became fused. He felt suspended between air and water, and various images began to move in and out of each element. He saw Emma coming out of the water onto the ship's deck carrying a worn brown suitcase. She wore a wide-rimmed, banded straw hat, a cream, long-sleeved, high-neck dress, white gloves, and black shoes. Her clothing, like the suitcase, had seen better days. She'd arrived at his compound one day in April. A servant had come to announce her presence. Jaja was not expecting her. The heavy chains of office clunked as he rose from the leopard-skin mat, took up his staff, and went outside. The sun was a brass plaque in the sky. He took in his visitor in one sweeping glance but said nothing.

'I am Emma White,' she said and removed her right glove. Jaja shook her proffered hand, but remained wordless, calmly observing the young woman before him.

'I come from Monrovia. Here is my letter of recommendation.'

Jaja reached out his hand and silently began reading the letter, which was signed by his Liberian friend, Sao Benson.

'You welcome,' he said. 'I admire your President, Joseph Jenkins Roberts.' Jaja turned sideways and gestured for her to enter the hut. Some women stood with wondering eyes outside other huts in the compound. A group of children were playing a clapping game.

The slightly shabby appearance of the woman from Liberia did not hide from Jaja the strength he saw in her hoist of the suitcase, in her erect posture and in her fierce eyes. He called one of his wives to take good care of the visitor. This meant a bush bath, fresh clothes, a newly-made bed, and food. When Jaja asked for Emma later that day, the wife who'd taken care of her said she'd fallen asleep around four o'clock and was still fast asleep. Emma did not wake again until the morning's cocks started crowing. Around mid-morning, after everyone had eaten, Jaja sat alone with her.

'Who be your people? Where you place?' he asked.

'I come from North America, a place called Arkansas. Came to Liberia ten years ago, two years after the American Civil War. Just a few hundred of us Blacks were there when I arrived. But I could not pass over the chance to live in a place where black men rule.'

'It is said Liberia best country for black man found on the face of earth.'

'Yes,' Emma said smiling, her hands folded on her knees. 'We value education highly. I hope I can be of some service to you in that regard.'

Jaja was impressed by her fluency in English and by her poise. His own reading and writing skills at this time were rudimentary; she could help him as his personal coach. He thought a moment longer and said, 'We have school run by Mistuh Gooding a'ready. You make good secretary too, but Mistuh Williams is secretary a'ready.' She remained calm, poised, looking down at her folded hands.

'You welcome,' Jaja said. 'You can stay here. I will find place fo' you. You be housekeeper, governess, and my coach in English language, if you want.'

'That would be very kind of you, King Jaja. I would be honoured,' Emma said.

'You welcome,' Jaja said, laughing. Since it would be clear to all from the way she dressed and spoke that she was not from Opobo, Jaja asked Emma to use his last name as a way of protecting her. As a result, rumours began to spread that she had become one of his wives, though she never played that role. Emma gratefully accepted the king's offer, which bought her the freedom to travel all over the kingdom without fear or hindrance.

By the time she'd met and married an Opobo man named Johnson, she'd become an Opobian, on most occasions dressing like the other women, while retaining her western dress when she accompanied Jaja and his chiefs to meetings with European officials. She became a consummate diplomat.

She stayed with him, and he rewarded her. Eventually, when Mr. Williams and Mr. Gooding retired, Jaja made Emma his secretary and head of Opobo's elementary school. She had remained loyal to the end – the trial at Accra that doomed him to exile.

Another form unfurled through the air now, over the deck and along the hallway of his cabin dreams – Becka's. As he had been taught to read and write, he, in turn, had taught her some of what he knew. They were all one people, one family. He felt her hand on his, guiding it to just underneath the navel, and he felt something move like a pulse, a throb of life, a tiny jolt of recognition. It was enough to make him weep with joy. His Becka had risen to the sky above the tar-grey sea with its arcing dolphins. She had caught up with him as he steamed forward, homeward.

Becka said, 'Evuhting good, Jaja. Doan worry you head.'

'De British. They want to kill me. Till my foot touch Opobo soil, I never will believe what they say. I never will know peace.'

'We child kicking, Jaja. Tink 'bout we child.'

Becka had already finished the final cleaning of the house and was sitting in the public room with her bags packed, when Mr. Brathwaite arrived around midday. It was the Friday following Jaja's departure. She received her wages and placed the money in her pocketbook. Mr. Brathwaite offered to drop her off in Jordan's tenantry on his way home. The remains of brown fronds sighed in the harvested cane fields, although little green rattoon shoots had already broken the soil like new-borns eager to enter the world. She'd be glad to see her mother and sister. She'd be glad to be home.

Mr. Brathwaite said, 'I am terribly sorry for you, Becka, and much saddened by Jaja's fate. I really am. I know how important he was to you.'

'Thank you, Mistuh Brathwaite.'

'Now that he's gone, did he ever tell you who helped him try to escape?' Becka's face hardened like a sea-rock. Mr. Brathwaite continued. 'I promise I won't tell anyone and you won't get into any trouble.'

'No, Mistuh Brathwaite. He didn't tell me a t'ing.'

Mr. Brathwaite opened and closed his mouth without saying anything.

'I have been much impressed with your work at Walmer's, Becka, and I am sorry it had to end, especially in this manner. I would like you to work for me at Jordan's Great House.'

'Dah is alright, Mr. Brathwaite. But I got a job a-ready.'

'Where? With whom?'

'De Hanschells. Judge Hanschell and he wife. I goin' be their maid from Monday.'

'Well, that is just splendid, Becka. Just splendid. Clearly there is no need for my recommendation. But if you ever were to need one, you won't hesitate to ask, will you?'

'Thank you, Sir.'

Silence rose between them. She thought she'd overcome this discomfort around white men. Over the past three months she'd regularly been in their presence: the First Secretary, John Cheeks, the doctors, the Hanschells, and even Mr. Brathwaite himself, who'd stayed over at Walmer's for a few nights. While she had grown more comfortable around them, she had never been in such a close proximity as the sharing of a carriage seat. Suddenly, her old fears rose again. She swallowed her saliva in an effort to relax and to remain composed. It was the way he'd looked at her when he said, "won't hesitate" as if she owed him something, as if he wanted something from her in the guise of making her an offer. Patsy's stories, and her own instincts remained inside her like a bedrock of limestone. She recalled again how, from time to time, some girl whom she'd played with in the tenantry cart-roads, had made the journey to become a live-in maid at a plantation house, and returned to the village with a hanging head, dour eyes and a stomach swollen with a child by the planter or one of his sons. She had been lucky. Mr. Brathwaite had spent little time at Walmer Cottage, so he had not been tempted as much as if he had been seeing her every day. That, and the presence of the king, had saved her. But she would have to keep her guard up at the Hanschells. She would keep the phial of oleander juice at hand. The thought made her start to cough. She said nothing more for the rest of the journey. When the carriage stopped by the track that ran through the tenantry, she jumped out with her bags and bolted along it like a mare. She didn't look back. As she ran, she remembered how Worrell had attacked her that day at Walmer's on her return from St. Barnabas Church. She ran even faster. In the end, it wasn't white men alone who had to be feared. Just men. Only one man had claimed her trust. Only one had inspired her affections and shown the meaning of love. Her thoughts hovered over the ship, wishing to guide him safely home.

Frances was taking clothes off the line when Becka rushed into the yard. Panting, she dropped her bundle and sat on it.

'Becka! You awright?' Frances asked.

'I good.' Becka rose from her seat, fanning her face with both hands. They hugged and looked at each other, hands resting on the other's shoulders.

Frances lowered her gaze and said, 'Like you put on a lil' weight.' She placed a hand on Becka's stomach, and they both laughed. Becka didn't have to tell her who the father was.

'O God,' Becka said. 'I suh glad to see you.'

'Wuh happen?' Frances asked. 'I know you.' So they went inside and Becka told her about Jaja's attempted escape, his recapture, his worsening health, his departure for Africa. She wept as she recounted the events, and Frances wept with her.

'But I got some good news too,' Becka said. 'I start wukking wid de Hanschells from Monday. They live next door to Walmer Cottage.'

'But wuh 'bout de child?'

'Shouldn' be nuh problem.'

'Well, when de time come, you drop you baby hey. I tek care of it fuh you. But you hold on to you job.'

'How Ma?'

'Not good.'

'Wuh you mean, "Not good"?'

'She ain' doing good at-all.'

Becka rose and went quietly to the bedroom doorway. She opened the curtain and saw that her mother was sleeping. She stepped softly inside, knelt beside the bed, and gently rubbed her mother's hand. When she rejoined Frances, they looked at each other with a sense of the inevitable. Their mother had struggled and suffered long. It was time to let her go. Frances would look after Becka's baby during the week, and Becka would contribute as much of her wages as she could and come home at weekends. Hopefully, Fred would continue sending money from Panama.

Early on Saturday morning, Becka went to check on her mother and found her lying peaceful and motionless. She placed her cheek on her mother's face but did not feel any breath.

Next day, a long line of villagers gathered in the wooded area that used to be the slave graveyard. Now, there were a variety of mature trees including a stately mastic, flamboyant, rodwood, mahogany, and clammy-cherry. A thick skin of dried and drying leaves covered the area which stood about half a mile from the plantation house and just less than a quarter of a mile from where the slave quarters used to be.

Becka's mother had passed on the stories and images of the old life as told to her by her mother. In the old days, the dead person was placed in a rectangular or diamond-shaped box held together by nails, and the grave was decorated with seashell trinkets, broken clay pots or bottles. Clothing and jewellery was placed in the casket, and the body aligned so the head was to the west and the feet to the east, so they wouldn't have to turn around when Gabriel blew his trumpet in the east. After the burial, mourners scattered shells and pottery on top of the grave mound. These days, the villagers still honoured their ancestors with these ceremonies in the woods where their ancestors's bones lay, but now the practice of decorating the graves and burying the dead with jewellery or tobacco pipes, anything thought of as an African practice, was not allowed by the churches. Only flowers placed on top of the casket were permitted. And even those Blacks who'd been baptized at the St. George Parish Church were still buried in an area separate from the Whites. Unbaptized Blacks received a poor person's burial in a public area allocated by the government.

Becka's uncle Ossie led the assembly to a large mastic tree in the old slave burial ground. In his brown felt hat and black velvet jacket, he led the hymns that battled with the sound of the wind. As they sang, from time to time, blackbirds perched in the mastic's branches soared from their green rooms in search of food. There, under the canopy of shade, Ossie gave thanks and praises to God and the ancestors, and those gathered before him responded with 'Hallelujahs' and 'T'ank yuh, Jesus'. Then, because Frances had become choked with grief, he called on Becka to say a few words.

She said, 'When I come up Friday evening, Ma did talking, though she did hoarse, and complaining of a pain in she chest. But before she went sleep, she summon she energy and pelt she hands round me and Frances' neck. She kissed both o' we and den she shut she eye and went sleep. De Lord got she now. Nuh more suffering fuh she. One day, we all gine see she on the other side. Thank God, we ain' gine always live hey.' Becka broke into sobs and looked as if she was about to fall. Her uncle steadied her while Frances and a few of the other women consoled her.

Uncle Ossie ran a finger over his grey moustache. Lifting both hands, he thanked God for His blessings and for the life of his dear sister, Juliet. He looked toward the oxcart that carried her remains in a plain diamond-shaped deal-board box, and then he signalled for the procession to begin its journey. He led the oxcart along the dirt track, the sun glinting through spaces in the trees, the blackbirds, sparrows, and wood doves chirping cheerfully.

Behind the oxcart, scores of men, women and children followed, with hymns and chants, accompanied by the tuk musicians positioned in the middle of the procession. They beat out a solemn march called a fassie, notes to wing the mother's spirit to her ancestral place. The martial notes of the snare rang out and the bass drummer struck one side of his drum with a stick with cloth tied around its end and the other side with his open left hand... *boom-boom boom boom, boom-boom boom boom, boom-boom boom boom...* The players' upper bodies swayed in vigorously, but their instruments remained upright and their hands were steady on the skins. The procession soon arrived at the cemetery and, after they'd sung a few more hymns, Ossie and three other men lowered Mrs. Jordan's body into the earth.

CHAPTER TWENTY-SEVEN

Though joint-pains, especially in his knees, still assaulted him, Jaja became steady enough to walk about his cabin for slightly longer periods. Several times each day, the ship's doctor came to administer his medicines. Jaja waited rigid as a man with a gun pressed to his temple, fearful that one of the injections, with Queen Victoria's approval, would send him to another world. His fear was made worse when the doctor sedated him to bring him some rest. It was with relief that he woke in the morning for another living day. He tried to raise his spirits by reading and by fastening on to the happy thought of reaching Opobo, of imagining its earth underfoot. This kept his mind alert and his heart flickering with hope. Even if he went to his ancestors as soon as he disembarked from his canoe on the Opobo waterfront, just arriving there would gladden his heart. He was not afraid of death; it was the thought of dying in a foreign country, of his soul's rejection by the ancestral spirits who would not be able to recognize him, to take him in. When an officer came to tell him the *Comus* was about to pull into harbour, Jaja exclaimed like an excited ox, almost injuring himself in his haste to rise from the bed and knocking over the oil lantern that stood on the bedside table. Hearing the noise, the young officer came in to help him up, handed him his cane, and, at the king's request, escorted him over to the porthole. Jaja looked towards the coastline and saw a beach that stretched along a bay. He saw buildings, some in clear view, others partially hidden by trees. Mountains rose behind the buildings and the silhouettes of other distant peaks stretched behind them like echoes.

'This… is not… Africa!' Jaja bellowed. He doubled over and

fell on his side. The officer tried to help him up, but Jaja wouldn't budge. The officer left and returned with the ship's doctor and together they carefully hoisted Jaja up and steered him back onto the bed. After the doctor determined Jaja was all right, he and the officer left the room.

Jaja felt his spirits plunging into darkness again. He wept silently. When the other passengers had disembarked, two officers came for Jaja and lowered him and Oko Jumbo down the side of the vessel into a waiting row-boat. Two officers came down the rope ladder to join them, and the local boatsmen began guiding the boat toward the shore. As they started towards the pier, Jaja looked up at the steamship and saw the Captain and an officer about to descend into another row-boat.

Jaja called out, 'What am I doing here? This not Nigeria.'

The officers looked at each other but remained silent. Then one of them said, 'There was a last-minute change of plans to stop here. If you need further details you will have to speak with the Captain.'

'Where are we?'

'Santa Cruz, Tenerife. We're in the Canary Islands.'

'What this mean? I must go to Opobo. I must go to my people.' Jaja leaned hard on his cane.

The officer was about to respond but hesitated, until he said, 'We're here to pick up the new British Consul to the Niger Delta. When he arrives from England, we will continue on to Africa. We're just eighty miles away from its north-western tip. I cannot say any more.'

Jaja stared at the officer. He wasn't angry with him. He was grateful that he had risked rebuke from his superiors by giving him the information. He just kept thinking, *Further delays. More delays.* He was convinced the British wanted him dead and this was their bloodless way to do it. What more did they want from him? They had told him not to expect reinstatement as King of Opobo, and he had 'agreed' to be compliant to British designs in the Delta. Did they realise that none of the pledges he made to them were legally binding? He had been tried in Accra, a place which had no jurisdiction over him, a king of a sovereign country. But this was of little consolation as Jaja felt his strength leaking away like the last dribbles of oil down the trunk of a palm tree. They knew him. They knew he would never stop fighting, knew that if ever an opportunity came for restoring his kingship, he would seize it. Eighty more miles to the tip, then south along the coast to Bonny and the creek that would lead him home. But how long would this delay be? Who could believe anything the British said?

They reached the waterfront and waited for the boat carrying the captain to arrive. When everyone had gathered on the dock, the captain led them to the long wooden customs shed to take care of the paperwork.

Tourism had recently begun in Tenerife, its operations centred here at Santa Cruz. A local businessman, who operated the island's carriage service, had opened one of the city's first hotels, Camacho's Hotel. He ran it with his English wife, Penelope, and it was there that Jaja would be staying.

An officer walked alongside the king while the other officer moved ahead to flag down a carriage. Soon, the horse and pair began moving along the streets cobbled with squares of volcanic rock. Through the window, Jaja looked for trees he recognized. He saw frangipanis and flamboyants, bananas and sisal. There were others he'd never seen before that he found appealing, that sparkled with red and white floral clusters. He noted the intricately-designed finishes to the iron-railed balconies on each floor of the city's buildings. Beyond the palms and flamboyant trees he caught sight of the rolling lines of the distant mountains, like some grey-hided creature.

The carriage slowed as it moved inland, away from the port. The gradual and continuous ascent made the vehicle creep along, though it took only twenty minutes to reach the hotel, which squatted about a mile away at the foot of a mountain. As soon as Jaja reached his hotel room, he undressed and soon fell asleep.

Around nine in the morning, he heard a knock on the door. Slowly, he got out of bed and put on his robe. The door swung open and a woman came in. She blushed and began miming that she would bring him food to eat. Jaja tried to laugh but his pains permitted only a wan smile. The woman smiled, then wordlessly left the room. Soon, she returned with his breakfast.

She said, 'Soy Teresa.' Her teeth sparkled. Her thick middle-aged arms and legs were solid and burnished a light bronze.

He said, 'I am Jaja. You speak English?'

Teresa shook her head and said, 'No ingles. No ingles.' She placed the tray on the table beside his bed. He looked at the food: scrambled eggs and bacon, plain rolls, mint tea, porridge and bananas. He nodded at Teresa who smiled again as she left.

An hour or so later, the Captain came to Jaja's room to inform him of what he already knew, and of more specific news. In two days the new consul for the Niger delta, Mr Claude MacDonald, was expected to join the *Comus* for the journey to Nigeria. Jaja thanked him for the information.

Jaja looked around the sparsely furnished hotel room. Apart from the cane chair and its twin on the other side of the room, there was only a centre table and a side table on which were placed clusters of candles. There were two oil paintings on the walls. In one, two women stood near a tree in a meadow with patches of flowers and a nearby lake. Four children in yellow, orange, and blue dresses accompanied the women, themselves in white and blue long-sleeved, high-necked cotton dresses, each carrying an umbrella. In the second painting, there was a woman in an orange-coloured dress and a child in white. They appeared to be searching the meadow for something, perhaps looking for flowers to place in the wicker basket hanging from the woman's arm.

The paintings triggered images of Becka in his mind. She dressed like these women when she went shopping in the city. He saw her in her bonnet, but carrying no umbrella, needing her hands for the groceries she carried. The paintings evoked her love of the outdoors and the way the island breezes seemed to cup her body. He could almost smell the herb garden on the eastern side of Walmer Cottage that wafted its minty perfumes through each room. Would he ever see her again? Moved by these thoughts, he got up and opened the wide-louvred door onto the hotel's gardens. He swung it open in a decisive gesture, as if he was emerging from his palace to address the people.

Tenerife's sea breezes charged in, temperate and refreshing, and the songs of birds greeted him. He recognized the chirps of goldcrest, sparrow, and pigeon. A robin arced through the garden.

He took in the profusion of palms and what looked like ever-greens with tiny leaves and clusters of little yellow flowers. Two baby royal palms erupted near the base of the evergreens and behind them the mountain crouched confident and still, stark in the mid-morning light.

CHAPTER TWENTY-EIGHT

A week or so into the second stage of her pregnancy, Becka saw Jaja. She glimpsed him one morning in late June as she was dusting off a mat in the Hanschells' side porch, which faced the south side of Walmer Cottage. She saw him through a space in the line of royal palms and flamboyants that separated the two properties. His hand gently rested on the tree's trunk, and he was looking directly at her. They made eye contact, and Becka dropped the mat and ran to him. 'Jaja! Jaja!' When she reached the fence, no-one was there. Her eyes darted everywhere. She stretched over the fence and craned her neck in every direction but saw only the empty driveway. She stood looking at the house, its louvres covering the window sashes behind them, louvred doors protecting the ones behind them, the FOR SALE sign planted in the circular garden bed near the front porch, bursting with weeds and allamandas' bright yellow bells. Everything she saw was as hard and stark as sunlight, but her heart told her that the king was still alive.

The Hanschells knew that Becka was being taunted by people in the neighbouring villages who knew of her relationship with the king. This, coupled with her pregnancy, softened Mrs. Hanschell to the point that she allowed Becka time to rest in her room whenever she needed to do so. Someone had invented a song, and everyone, from the small children to the aged, sang its chorus, especially when they passed her on the street:

> King Jaja won' leh Becka 'lone,
> King Jaja won' leh Becka 'lone,
> King Jaja won' leh Becka 'lone,
> Wha' Becka got, um is all she own.

Becka would hold her shoulders erect and her head high in the face of such teasing, which was sometimes malicious. A woman had pointed at her belly and asked, 'So when de prince comin'? He gine be de next King Jaja?' Her loud cackling laughter had followed her into the Hanchells' front yard. Becka remained straight and proud as a royal palm, but sometimes, in the privacy of her room, she wept – from the ridicule and from her longing. One thing was certain. She wouldn't hide the knowledge of Jaja from the baby. She was proud of her association with him; the child would know of its kingly heritage and of its conception from love.

When Becka went into town, which was now weekly, she would go to the Central Ice House hoping to see John Cheeks and get some news about Jaja. But each time she went there she was told that John wasn't in the office. This went on for weeks. She thought of going to Fontabelle to find him. Jaja had told her that this was where John lived. But she quickly dismissed this idea, knowing how dangerous it would be for her to go into that exclusive residential area, unaccompanied and without permission. She searched the weekly newspapers at the Hanschell's for any news of Jaja, but they yielded nothing.

Towards the end of June, she decided to try the Central Ice House again. As she entered the building, the front-desk clerk looked up and frowned with recognition.

She said, 'It's you again?' Becka steeled herself, but before she could say anything, the woman disappeared into the back of the room and returned with a middle-aged white man in a suit and tie. The man, whom she assumed to be the manager, said, 'This is a place of business. We have already told you a thousand times that Mr. Cheeks no longer works here. You are disrupting our business. If you come in here again, I will have you arrested for loitering. Do you understand?'

Becka turned and left the building. Halfway down the steps, she heard a voice behind her whispering loudly, 'You! You!' Turning, she saw a brown woman in a white cotton dress. Becka stepped into the street, stopped, and waited. The woman looked around in all directions, as if checking there were no witnesses to her pursuit. 'Wait! Wait!' she said, catching up with Becka. She placed a hand on Becka's shoulder and guided her to the side of the building.

'I see you come hey evuh week, and I hear how ruff Mr. Hutchinson talk you down just now. Wuh you want?'

Becka told her.

The woman said, 'He ain' only not wukking hey nuh-more. Mister Cheeks ain' even in de island. He mudder dead a few weeks ago, so he left de island and living in New York wid he uncle. When she dead, it like he drop evuhthing and cut and run. He ain' waste nuh time a-tall in leaving de place.'

Becka stared at the woman. 'How you know all dis?'

'Yuh does hear a lotta things when yuh cleaning and moving 'bout in dey.' The woman resumed her furtive glancing around. Becka kept her eyes closely focused on the woman's face, wondering whether what she said was truth or rumour. The woman glanced around again as if some unseen power was urgently summoning her. Suddenly and wordlessly, she fled.

Inside the grocery shop near the Ice House, Becka bought some salted cod, a few tins of sardine, salt-bread, and cornmeal. She did this without thinking and was hardly aware of the other patrons as she moved towards the cashier with her purchases. Her mind was still trying to digest what she'd heard. She knew John would have been terrified of being implicated in the escape plot, and she wondered if the woman had got her facts right. Had it been John's departure from the island that had killed his aging mother and not him leaving because of his mother's death?

It was the hard sunlight pressing on her face that put her feet back on the ground.

She watched a man in a worn jacket and ragged brown felt hat steering his donkey cart along Roebuck Street, saw him looking behind to check that the lengths of wood projecting like a stiff tail from the back of the cart were still there. The Friday streets steadily grew with traffic and people, mainly women shopping for their mistresses and themselves.

She felt the weight of the child growing inside her, and wondered who it would most resemble. She hoped it would look more like Jaja, be a constant reminder of him. She would take the child with her wherever she went: to the city, to church, to her friends' houses. Jaja would always be with her.

When she reached the bottom of Two Mile Hill, she stopped to get a cup of mauby from a vendor seated on a box next to the barrel that contained the drink. She withdrew a glass cup from inside the box, walked to the front of the barrel and turned the tap.

After Becka finished drinking, the vendor took the glass from her and said, 'You like you real thirsty.' She placed the glass under the tap again and poured a second cup of the bittersweet frothing drink. Becka drank again and then handed over enough coins to cover the cost of the two drinks. The vendor returned half of the money, pressing the coin into Becka's palm and folding her fingers around it.

'You unly ha' tuh pay me for one, Becka. I know who you is. De extra drink fuh de lil' one yuh carrying.'

Becka thanked her, blessed her, and continued up the hill.

CHAPTER TWENTY-NINE

Five days had passed since Consul MacDonald's supposed arrival in Tenerife, and Jaja's mistrust of Britain was a shark endlessly circling around him. Around eleven o'clock, a knock sounded on his door, which had been left unlocked because of the delicate state of his health. The ship's captain entered with Mr. Camacho. Jaja, who was sitting up in bed, lowered the book he was reading about the ancient history of Tenerife onto his lap.

The Captain asked how he was feeling.

'How you expect me feel?'

The Captain ignored this response and said, 'There has been a delay in our consul's arrival from England, and I'm sorry to have to inform you of further bad news. There has been an outbreak of dysentery in Tenerife, and it's island-wide. This means our ship has been quarantined and will further delay the consul's arrival. We have no choice but to wait-out the epidemic.' The Captain abruptly left the room, Mr. Camacho following him, glancing back at Jaja with his sad, doe-like eyes.

Was the captain telling the truth? Was this just another lie, another deliberate attempt to prevent his return? It was the uncertainty that made him so anxious. Why didn't they just shoot him like a soldier and let him go to his ancestors? He knew the answer to that question. The British had to appear blameless in the eyes of the world. They would silence him by letting him die from his ailments and his grief. This was what the delaying tactics were about. Jaja felt his spirit turn restlessly. He drew the caned chair to the door that opened out into the garden. To the left, a white frangipani (was that what Becka called it?), to the right, a large leafy evergreen with round green nuts or fruits rustled under the grey-blue sky. He could see the massive shoulders of the mountain. Drenched in sunlight, small palms, bougainvillea, and some red flowering trees and vines dotted its lower slopes. The wind rippled the leaves in the garden. A fringe of cloud coasted from behind the top of the mountain.

Jaja remained watching, thinking how the heat would have softened on the other side of the mountain, as breezes came in from the bay. The side of the mountain facing him became incandescent in the sun. Jaja got up to close the drapes against the harshness of the light. As he did so, he felt faint, seized by vertigo, as if something was snatching control away from him. He remained still for a while to catch himself. When the dizziness subsided he saw that the mountainside was now completely lit and an even greater variety of green and brown shrubs was now visible on its stern face. He saw a horizontal vein or scar running across the mountain, about one-thirds down from its peak, and underneath it what looked like a window or square mouth of a cave. How might he reach there? He knew he couldn't climb that mountain, yet there had to be a way. He imagined taking refuge in the cave and surviving for as long as necessary by eating, under night's blanket, whatever fruit and leaves he found there. Then, when the authorities assumed he was dead, he would make his way to the port and find a vessel bound for Africa.

He fell into a long reverie. When he awoke from this half-sleep a few hours later, the sun had dipped behind a cluster of clouds. He watched the mountains turn to silhouette. He knew he wouldn't sleep tonight. The thought of being buried in foreign soil took all peace from him.

The following Saturday, nine days after MacDonald had been expected to arrive, Jaja snapped out of his trancelike state and told one of the officers of his desire to go for a stroll along the beach. This would help him sleep better: the fresh air, the exercise, the water's peaceful lapping. The doctor advised him to remain indoors.

'I am Jaja, king of sovereign country. I demand to be allowed to leave dis prison of a room.' Jaja flayed his arms in the air.

The doctor stared at him as if deciding whether to try to

convince him to remain indoors for his own good, or to just flee from the room.

'You may go,' the doctor said with a sigh, 'but on one condition.'

'And what might that be?'

'Someone will need to escort you. You are still a very sick man. You have lost a considerable amount of weight. It would be unwise for you to go out unaccompanied, even if the Captain permits it.'

Jaja nodded. This was a reasonable compromise. When the doctor returned, presumably after talking to the Captain, he was accompanied by two of the ship's officers who waited outside Jaja's door until he got dressed. When he was ready, the officers escorted Jaja to the carriage in front of the hotel. In fifteen minutes they were at the beach-front, and Jaja got out, cane in hand, with Oko Jumbo at his heels. The two officers stood under a large evergreen that resembled a weeping willow, although more of its trunk was visible. Jaja felt the officers' eyes on him as he slowly made his way up the sandy shore. Tongue-lolling, Oko repeatedly ran ahead and of him and then ran back to meet him. The beach in the sheltered bay stretched no more than a couple hundred yards.

Thereafter, twice a week, under the officers' surveillance, Jaja took a stroll along the palm-lined, pebbled strip, sometimes stopping to turn south-west towards Becka, and then south-eastward in the direction of Africa. But three weeks later, there was still no improvement in his heart and respiratory condition, and there was still no word of when the ship would leave. MacDonald still hadn't arrived. Jaja's weight had dropped to a mere one hundred and twenty pounds, and he was aware of the increased effort it took him to walk a short distance even with the assistance of his cane.

Each day Jaja felt weaker and more listless. Once, he looked at himself in the hotel mirror and hardly recognized what he saw there. He had shrunk to less than half his normal size. The doctor urged him to remain in his hotel room, but Jaja was determined to assert his independence, fight to stay alive and to make it home.

He was on the beach. He started and stopped, crept and paused.

Suddenly, another dizzy spell seized him. But this time, the grip was firmer, and he couldn't shake it off. He heard Oko Jumbo bark sharply. A shadow that had fallen across both of them. He was losing consciousness when he felt a hand on his shoulder and a charge of energy coursing through his body. He looked up at a tall, long-haired man holding a pole in his left hand. The pole was at least one-and-a-half times the man's height. He wore pigskin leather sandals and a skirt with a decorative waistband made of what looked like wool. A goatskin cape, draped over his left shoulder and held in place by a cord that ran under his right arm, reached to his knees. He carried an animal-hide bag, its strap running across his chest, the bag resting on his right hip. His moustache was thick, beard thin; he had shoulder-length black hair. His imposing muscular body was tan coloured, and his features looked both European and African, perhaps from north-ern Africa. Was this man a priest of some kind? He stood erect, his robe draped in the same manner as his own when he assumed the role as high priest of the Ikuba Oracle.

'Guanche,' the man said in a voice filled with volcanic rock. Then he removed his hand from the king's shoulder.

'Guanche,' he repeated. He moved closer to the voice and to the forefinger which the speaker pointed towards his chest. Then, Guanche gestured for him to come even closer.

'Jaja,' he said, placing a finger on his own chest and looking up at the hairy mountain of a man. Then the man stooped with his back to him, tapped his shoulder and beckoned to him. The energy which he had felt coming from Guanche's touch did not diminish. He understood the invitation and mounted the stranger's back. Guanche rose with his burden and headed toward the mountain face, the same one he saw from Camacho's hotel.

When they reached the foot of the mountain and started to ascend, he was sure that Guanche intended to take him to the black eye-socket that he had seen from his hotel door and had dreamt of escaping to, there to survive on nature's providence until night's dark hand led him away from this place to Opobo. Excitement grew in him like a yam root. But when they reached the dark entrance, Guanche passed it by without a look and sped up to the mountain's crest. From there, he saw the northern range with peaks far higher than the one on which they stood. Guanche had not used his pole before, but now, as they headed north, he had to do so. He clung tightly to Guanche's back as he vaulted over the brown and grey gullies, crevices and ravines, the rock seams horizontally stitching the mountains' faces, the deep gorges that became gushing waterways during heavy rainfall. They passed the sparse vegetation and the greener more forested areas mottling the slopes, passed mountain goats and sheep, shepherds and their wolf hounds. In the distance, mist coiled and blended with the clouds. Over the hard, grey-black, volcanic mountain's thighs and shoulders, he touched down and soared, touched down and soared on Guanche's back.

As they continued, the mist grew thicker, rising from the valleys like steam. Near the tops of the ridges, propelled by the wind, it careened into the clouds, became clouds. Guanche moved in and out of the white and grey fog like a great bird sweeping and arcing along the rocky verges. Up ahead, the mist assumed a numinous brightness, as it churned up between the mountains.

A final vault put them in a clearing hedged with short palms near the widening end of a ravine. Women who carried water in clay jars up the slope reminded him of his own womenfolk making their way back to the compound from the springs or water holes. Some children pulsed about in noisy play, jumping with their poles, jostling with wooden toy spears, and throwing pebbles at each other. Preparing for their futures in war, he thought. He could see the dark mouths of caves dotting the mountain's slopes, and the sound of a dog's bark echoed around him. As Guanche continued up the slope, he looked across the path before them and saw a small circular area marked off around the base of a palm tree. Three groups of stones had been arranged within the circle, and containers of food sat between each cluster. This must be a public shrine, no doubt used by the villagers. As it was in Opobo, everyone here had access to the mouth of god.

When they reached a clearing further up the mountain, in front of a cave, Guanche stooped and let him down. He watched Guanche place his right index and middle fingers into his mouth, breathe deep, and release a soaring whistle that was at once piercing and melodic. It echoed through the valley and, in seconds, a group of men, women, and children emerged from the cavern with smiles and greetings, the children all naked, the young and adult women in soft animal skins reaching from neck to calf, hair plaited or falling freely to their shoulders, wearing necklaces of clay beads, seashells, pebble and bone. Guanche led him into the cave where women were laying out food in ceramic and wooden bowls on a table carved from the rock face. He saw goat cheese and roasted mutton, figs and dates, fish and other meats, jugs of milk and wine.

Someone handed him a plate and said, 'Gofio.' He took it. It was flat and roasted, like some type of bread. Everyone looked at him with buzzing anticipation and in their smiles he recognized his own code of hospitality, the same smiles which his people unfurled in the breaking and sharing of kola nut. The bread tasted of barley, wheat and beans, all mixed together and warm on his tongue. Each time he swallowed a piece of it, the bread's pleasurable taste drew laughter from his mouth, and he felt his spirits lifting higher. His new friends joined in his delight and surrounded him with their own mirth. After he'd eaten his fill, a young man took him outside and led him to a natural spring where an elderly woman gave him a mineral bath. He didn't understand any of their language, but hand and head gestures that said *Follow me, Over there, This way, You are friend, I understand* did well enough.

Next morning, he woke to the sound of a blown conch shell. Guanche soon appeared and beckoned him to follow. Outside, the morning air cool, he shivered and clasped his arms tightly around his body. Soon a boy appeared with a woollen cape. Across the face of the mountain, families poured out of their caves. Guanche withdrew the conch from his leather bag and blew a message whose tone was plaintive, elegiac. His household advanced solemnly to a large clearing that other villagers were approaching and where some of them had already assembled. No one had yet eaten their morning meal. From the outpouring of sorrow and the large gathering, it was evident that some noble person must have died. Judging from Guanche's role in the proceedings, he believed the dead person must have been a close relative, like a father or father-in-law. Guanche addressed the crowd and their weeping and moaning broke across the mountain and echoed through the valleys. After this brief speech, everyone filed slowly back to their dwellings on the slopes.

He followed Guanche into an area of the cave where a young man and several adult men and women had gathered around something. As they approached the group, the young man suddenly rose and turned around. He held a cloth that contained what looked like bloody human organs. He placed the dripping collection in a wicker basket. With eyes fixed far beyond their immediate surroundings, the youth sped out through the tunnel, moving as though his life depended on it.

He approached the area where the dead man lay. The women poured water from large clay jars into wooden basins and washed the body in slow careful movements. When the corpse had been thoroughly cleaned, other women and men took turns covering it with ointments that appeared to contain a variety of roots, plants, and minerals. He watched two men lift the body, and followed them as they took the corpse outside and placed it on a mat in direct sunlight. Each day, this process was repeated until the body was fully dry, and, on each of those days, the people's weeping and moaning swelled through the valleys.

His own people's rituals could last as long as thirty-two days when a king or paramount chief died. The afterlife was important to these people, too; that was clearly the reason for the elaborate preparation of the body and the long period of mourning.

Around noon, he watched as two men wrapped the corpse in skins and a woman painted identification marks on them. A powerfully-built female, who reminded him of Teresa in the hotel, sewed the skins to form a tight casing around the body.

Guanche pointed to the cadaver and said, 'Xaxo.' He wasn't sure if he meant that the person who formerly lived in the body was named Xaxo or if he was calling the body a mummy. It didn't really matter. 'Xaxo,' he said, and followed the two men into the cave where they placed the corpse on raised boards inside the family tomb. He watched in wonder and with a deep sense of connection as family members filed past to ring the body with offerings of pigs', goats', and sheep's teeth, limpet shells, spears, clay bowls full of gofio, decorative ceramic bowls, grinding stones, knives made of volcanic glass – all the things the dead would need in the other world.

Now he saw a corpse being taken to the special house in the king's compound where lay the remains of his ancestors. There, it lay in state for three days as swarms of people – the entire town save for those physically unable to come – came to grieve until dawn. He saw the large open-sided construction covered with palm fronds strapped to thick bamboo poles. Under it, hundreds of people were sitting in wooden chairs or on goatskin mats. Drummers were pounding taut goat and sheep skins that were oiled with their sweat. A lavish feast was laid out on wooden tables near the back of the shelter. On the tables, covered with white cloths, were stacks of calabashes and wooden plates; bowls of creamed yams, fish, and vegetables cooked in palm oil; red peppers floating in gravy; bowls of goat meat and thick black soup; fish dumplings and bush meat; and jars upon jars of palm wine. The children of the deceased, all dressed in white, danced and sang. Guests showered them with cowries. Then he saw the corpse being slowly lowered into the family tomb to the salute of guns that fired twenty-five times. Afterward, a large goat was slaughtered, its parts, still bright with blood, precisely cut in pieces and given to each of the deceased's children on platters of banana leaves.

For another thirty-two days, memories were released from the tongues of those who knew the dead person. A container made of raffia palms was carried by two men to the back of the compound where the spirit would leave on its journey to the other side. They fetched the spirit back so it might sit in its native surroundings on the shores of memory. The dead one's spirit had willingly entered the container. As the men brought it from the back of the compound, it rocked from side to side. It was alive. All was well. The men paused to steady themselves and the animated spirit. The spectators bawled with excitement and began to sing in acknowledgment of this truth.

> O coming home, coming home
> To the elders' outstretched arms.

O coming home, coming home
To your elders' warm embrace.

And now he sees Sunday welcoming the chiefs who approach the container of his spirit. Hands reach out to them proffering cowries or palm wine, kola nuts and alligator pepper. The chiefs' robes settle around them like colourful plumage as each one takes a seat. Then, starting with the eldest, each one rises to sound the praises of the dead.

A ram is brought forward and a knife plunged into its throat, then the insides are expertly removed and tossed into a large clay bowl. The blood is drained into another bowl, some of it spilling and dyeing the dirt floor beneath the shelter. Days and nights follow of nonstop eating and drinking in the presence of the living dead, the flame watcher's eyes bright and keen with kola, so the flame in the clay-pot at his feet never goes out. Every now and then, a watcher pours oil into the pot, and the spirit of the dead laughs, pleased to witness every moment of the celebration held in his name, in his honour.

On the morning of July 6, 1891, King Jaja stirred slowly in his hotel bed, whose sheets were soaked with his perspiration. With an aching hand, he removed the covering sheet and, with another enormous effort, managed to raise himself into a sitting position. The window drapes had not been fully drawn back, but, looking through the window, he could see the mountain's dark eyesocket blankly staring back at him. He wasn't aware of slipping into a semiconscious state or of slumping over onto his left side. During the course of the day, from time to time he heard footsteps in the room. On one occasion, he heard Teresa's voice, 'Señor Jaja? Señor Jaja?' Another time, the nasal voice of the captain reached him. But their movements were vague and distant as in a dream.

Early next morning, just before sunrise, Jaja heard Oko bark twice and then he saw the figure of a man who resembled his father summoning him with a commanding gesture.

CHAPTER THIRTY

In July Becka dreamt of Jaja's death and felt it confirmed a few weeks later when she kept seeing him more frequently than before. He'd come to the fence that ran between Stratford Lodge and Walmer Cottage and wave to her as she watered the plants on the side porch or shook out a mat on the yard grass. He'd be wearing one of his robes or his cotton shirt with the cowry design. She would immediately drop her watering can or mat and sprint toward the fence, only to see nothing. She heard nothing, either, save for the chattering of the flamboyants' long brown pods that shook like a man's teeth rattling from ague, or the hiss and swish of wind shaking the palm trees' fronds. She'd walk slowly back to the house, fingers interlocked on the top her head in a clutch of silent wailing.

Mrs. Hanschell seemed to understand her suffering and not once did she reprimand Becka when she withdrew for hours to the servant's room, or when a mat or floor wasn't completely swept. On more than one occasion, Becka saw her employer airing a room that had been overlooked by her. Becka's one hope was that Jaja had died in his beloved Opobo and not in some unfamiliar land with none of the comforts of death: the nearness of family, friends, and his ancestors' open arms. He'd had many sleepless nights worrying about the fate of his spirit, and this fear had been especially acute in the days following his capture, when Dr. Archer had released the alarming report of his diseased heart, lungs and kidneys.

Although she knew he was gone, Becka still yearned for some factual confirmation of Jaja's death. The cleaning woman at Central Ice House had said that John Cheeks was living in New

York City with his uncle. Becka had no way of contacting him, and it was likely that he didn't know anything at all. New York was located in the same country as Charleston, South Carolina. That was all she knew. Each week, she checked the Hanschells' newspapers, but none carried any news of Jaja and his fate. It was as though he had never even been on the island. The only public remembrance of the king came in the anonymous, mocking song. At first, the ditty was just a four-line chorus –

> King Jaja won' leh Becka 'lone
> King Jaja won' leh Becka 'lone
> King Jaja won' leh Becka 'lone
> Wha' Becka got, um is all she own.

but after some weeks in circulation, two verses had now been added:

> If you want to live in sin,
> Get a lil' house and put me in.
> But if yuh start to play de fool,
> Ah'll get a big stick and keep you cool.

> If you love me, treat me nice,
> And I will cook you peas and rice.
> But if yuh start to play de fool,
> Ah'll get a big stick and keep you cool.

The singers sung each verse in two voices as if it were she and Jaja in dialogue, negotiating the terms of their relationship. While at first she had been hurt by the song, she became less offended by it and began to infuse it with her own significance and truth, even though she knew it had been composed with mischief and perhaps even malice in mind. She would have liked to engage with them, to find an opening through which the full and true story of Jaja's life and exile could be told. But she feared that there were few people who had any desire to hear Jaja's story, that most were satisfied to reduce this great man's life to a humorous folk song.

Becka's child was born on Thursday, December 10. She named her Grace Sarah Jordan and had her christened at St. George Parish Church. It wasn't until 1949, when she was 76 years old, that Becka at last heard something about Jaja in an article written by a man called E. M. Shilstone that appeared in *The Advocate* newspaper. The content of the article didn't surprise her. It began:

> 'A change of policy towards tribal taxation occasioned a review of Jaja's case, whereupon he was pardoned and given permission to return to his native land.'

Becka shook her head, recognizing the imperial language of diplomacy aimed at preserving the image of the Crown. It was still the language of all the Barbados newspapers, except the more liberal *Times*. She knew that if there was any credit to be given for the shortening of Jaja's term of exile, it was due to those good doctors, led by Dr. Archer, who gave a bleak and honest report on the state of Jaja's health. The last paragraph of the article brought her to tears, because it confirmed what she had known for fifty-eight years, but which she had never been able to confirm.

> 'His body was embalmed and placed in a coffin with a glass front through which his features could be seen. In this condition, his remains were sent to Opobo for his people to gaze upon their departed chief, and for burial. A statue of the hero of the tribe stands in Opobo.'

But while confirming his death, the article raised further questions. It didn't say where Jaja had died. He must have died after leaving Barbados but not in Africa. From where were his remains sent to Opobo? Did he die when the ship docked in England? Or did he die on board the Africa-bound ship? He couldn't have died, been embalmed, and placed in a glass coffin whilst at sea. All the article confirmed was that Jaja did not return to Opobo alive. She lowered her head in sorrow and thought: *Dah is why I did keep seeing he all de time out dey by Walmer Cottage. He soul won' sleep.* She stored the article in the basket of newspaper clippings about Jaja which she'd collected during their three months together.

Twenty-two years later, Evelyn, her great-great-granddaughter, now seventeen and attending high school, read her a reprint of that same article in a 1971 edition of *The Advocate*. Becka was now 98 years old and partially blind. As a little child, Evelyn had squirmed in delight at Becka's stories of the African king who was a part of their family. In spite of the village gossip and ridicule that had made the rest of her generation disown Jaja, Becka had let all her descendants know about the king who had been murdered by the British Government and whom she had loved and whose blood ran in their veins. She had been faithful in doing this. But of all her family, Evelyn was the only child who ever asked about Jaja, and Becka found comfort in the child's interest. She knew this would ensure Jaja's ancestral presence in their memory. She slowly tapped her way into the bedroom with one of Jaja's ironwood canes, the last of the four he had left her. She rested the cane on the side of the bed and, with a hand on its edge, she eased herself to the floor. Once on her knees, she slowly poked the cane under the bed and eventually withdrew a covered, coconut-frond basket which she handed to young Evelyn.

AFTERWORD

I engaged in extensive research in the process of constructing this fictional narrative of the last four months of the life of the legendary King Jaja of Opobo, one of Africa's great kings. Jaja spent two-and-a-half of those four months in my homeland, Barbados. Courtesy requires that I name the main sources without which this story could not have been told: articles on Jaja that appeared in the newspapers – the *Barbados Herald*, the *Barbados Globe*, the *Barbados Times*, and *The Advocate* (Barbados); and in the book, *King Jaja of Opobo (1821-1891): His Life and his Times* by Sylvannus Cookey (1974).

Many thanks to the staff of the Barbados Archives Department, the Barbados National Trust, the Barbados Museum and Historical Society, the Barbados Library Service, and the Museo de la Naturaleza de Hombre and the Biblioteca Municipal in Santa Cruz, Tenerife, Canary Islands, for their gracious assistance.

It was at the Biblioteca Municipal where my suspicion that King Jaja had been effectively murdered or at least been allowed to die by the British Government, and his remains thrown into some grave in Tenerife was confirmed. History books tell us that after the ship carrying the king from Barbados docked at Santa Cruz, Tenerife, an island-wide outbreak of dysentery kept it in quarantine, and that Jaja died from complications after contracting the disease. Two books, *Estudio de las Grandes Epidemis en Tenerife (Siglos XV-XX)* by Ana María Díaz Peréz and Juan Gabriel de la Fuente Perdomo (Cabildo de Tenerife, 1990) and *Santa Cruz Bandera Amarilla, Epidemias y Calamidades (1494-1910)* by Luis Cola Benítez (Ayuntamiento Organismo Autonomo de

Cultura Santa Cruz de Tenerife, 1996) confirm there was no dysentery epidemic in Tenerife in 1891. Neither were there any announcements of Jaja's death or burial in the Tenerife papers, *La Opinion* (1890-1895), *Las Noticias* (1889-1892), nor the 1891 *Diario de Tenerife*. It was only when they were threatened by Jaja's chiefs with the curtailment of trade relations that Britain negotiated with the Spanish government to have Jaja's body disinterred and returned to Opobo.

By deliberately delaying the ship at Tenerife, the British Government allowed Jaja to die of the heart, liver and lung diseases he'd developed during his exile in the Caribbean. The story of a dysentery epidemic on Tenerife in the summer of 1891 was a concoction by Britain to achieve its objective: to prevent a living Jaja reaching Opobo.

Britain's culpability for the death of King Jaja is further supported by the fact that, in 1937, the British Parliament granted Jaja's descendants $11,420 in settlement of their 1887 claim against the king's kidnapping by the then acting vice-consul to the Niger Delta, Harry Johnston. As the novel indicates, a phony trial and the sentence of exile followed the kidnapping.

Anthony Kellman was born in Barbados in 1955, educated at Combermere School, at UWI (Cave Hill) and in the U.S. At eighteen he left for Britain where he worked as a troubadour playing pop and West Indian folk music on the pub and folk club circuit. During the 1980s, he returned to Barbados where he worked as a newspaper reporter, then worked part-time to pay his way through UWI (Cave Hill) where he did a BA in English and History. Afterwards he worked in PR for the Central Bank of Barbados, experiences which he drew on in writing *The Coral Rooms*. At this time he published two poetry chapbooks, *In Depths of Burning Lights* (1982) and *The Broken Sun* (1984), which drew praise from Kamau Brathwaite, among others.

In 1987 he left Barbados for the USA where he studied for a MFA degree in Creative Writing at Lousiana State University. After completing, he took a professorship at Augusta State University, Georgia (now Augusta University), where he is Emeritus Professor of English and Creative Writing. He finds considerable resonances between the Caribbean and the Southern states in the USA, which feed into his poetry.

In 1990 Peepal Tree published his third book of poetry, *Watercourse*, the novel *The Coral Rooms* (1994), *The Long Gap* (1996), *Wings of a Stranger* (2000), *Limestone* (2008) – the first published epic poem of Barbados, and written in Tuk verse forms, based on the rhythms of Tuk, Barbados' indigenous music – and *South Eastern Stages* (2012). A second novel, *The Houses of Alphonso*, was published in 2004. All his work has a powerful involvement with landscape, both as a living entity shaping peoples' lives and as a source of metaphor for inner processes. The limestone caves of Barbados have provided a particularly fertile source of inspiration.

ALSO BY ANTHONY KELLMAN

The Coral Rooms
ISBN: 9780948833533; pp. 102, pub. 1994; price: £6.95

Percival Veer has risen to the tenth floor of the Federal Bank of Charouga, has acquired a large and imposing house and a young and attentive wife. But satisfaction eludes him. Guilt over a past wrong begins to trouble him and a recurrent dream of caves disturbs his sleep. As Percy's inner world crumbles, he is gripped by an obsessive desire to explore the deep limestone caves of his island, dimly remembered from his boyhood. This gripping, poetic novel charts Percy's meeting with his spiritual guide, Cane Arrow, and his hallucinatory descent into the cave's depths.

'Realistic and dreamlike, explicit and mysterious... The descriptions are evocative & sensual. A compelling read.' – Carole Klein.

'A realistic and convincing portrait of self-loathing' – Wilson Harris.

The Houses of Alphonso
ISBN: 9781900715829; pp. 192, pub. 2004; price: £8.99

Barbadian-born Alphonso Hutson has lived in the USA for nearly sixteen years. But he cannot settle. He has dragged his long-suffering American wife, Simone, and their children from house to rented house. He has refused to share with her any real explanation for the complex feelings that drive him. But this time she has had enough of his 'sorry restlessness', refuses to move with him and threatens the end of their marriage. Only then is Alphonso forced into confronting the ghosts that propel his perpetual migrancy.

The ghosts lie in his native Barbados. There is the love, shame and guilt he feels for the dead parents whose funerals he failed to attend, and there is the mystery of the brother he has never seen, hidden away in an institution. All is complicated by his mixed feelings for his homeland. It is the place that still feeds his imagination, but as a boy from a Black working class family he has felt excluded from the class structures of a country still dominated by a privileged White minority.

Kellman combines a poetic exploration of Alphonso's personal journey into his past, with an acute engagement with racial and political issues of a country in the midst of turmoil as the old order is challenged.

Watercourse
ISBN: 9780948833373; pp. 64; pub. 1990; price: £5.99

The celebrated Martiniquan poet and novelist Edouard Glissant writes: '*Watercourse* is more than a collection of poems. It is the continual amazement evoked by Caribbean landscape: a single dialogue between the sea and the land… a song whose dazzling waves foam among the islands… Anthony Kellman's poetry has the strength and sweetness of vegetation with the power of progressively revealing to us the nature of the earth in which it grows.'

The Long Gap
ISBN: 9780948833786; pp. 64; pub. 1996; price: £6.99

The Long Gap is a passionate exploration of the Caribbean exile's need 'to go back/to clutch the roots of the word'. Writing out of the the fear of the 'gap' which can grow too long, Kellman engages with his Barbadian heritage as one which both sustains and drives to anger. In language which echoes the rhythms of the 'tuk' band and the 'scat of the guitar strum', he celebrates the traditions of resistance and creative invention, but excoriates the islands of cocaine, political corruption and subservience to external masters.

Bruce King writes: 'Tony Kellman is always trying something different… He is a serious poet and the various contradictions and affiliations found in his verse embody those of the Caribbean and, to generalise, most poetry. A formalist attracted towards, oral, folk and popular traditions, he also mixes the highly lyrical with dialect and the prose-like. I especially like his metaphors and patterns of sound. When reading these poems you feel that… here is one of our best younger poets.'

Wings of a Stranger
ISBN: 9781900715447; pp.   71; pub. 2000; price: £7.99

In the continuing rite of return to his native Barbados from longer and longer away, something has happened for Tony Kellman. No longer are these the alienated poems of *the long gap*, of belonging nowhere. With greater establishment in America has come, *on the wings of a stranger*, the capacity to embrace this past and to see wholly afresh what was once familiar and unremarked. Parallel to these poems of place, are those that explore new love and its power to heal.

As well as Barbados, there are poems set in worlds as different as sharecropping Georgia and Yorkshire, England. In all of them one hears Kellman's signal voice which combines his urbane capacity to 'hum forever simple pleasure' and the ecstatic vision of a poet who 'puts on the garment of praise' to 'retell our special story'.

Limestone
ISBN: 9781845230036; pp. 200; pub. 2008; price: £9.99

Limestone is the epic poem of Barbados and a major development in an indigenous Caribbean poetics. Drawing on the folk music of Tuk, Anthony Kellman invents his own forms of Tuk verse to write the story of his island from the destruction of the Amerindians to the present day.

Part one uses both invented characters and actual historical persons such as Bussa and Nanny Grigg, the leaders of the 1816 slave revolt, to explore the epic of loss, survival and reinvention in the lives of the African slaves. Part two is set in the post-emancipation period up to the twenty-first year of independence. Through the voices of those who led the struggle against colonialism – Samuel Jackman Prescod, Charles O'Neal, Clement Payne, Grantley Adams and Errol Barrow – Kellman explores their inner anguish over the slow pace of advance and the inevitable compromises with external power. And as the queues of would-be emigrants at the American consulate lengthen, the island asks: when a White business class still dominates the economy, who has benefited from the people's struggles of the past?

Part three is set at the end of the twentieth century and tells the stories of Livingston, a young musician, and Levinia, an Indian-African Barbadian schoolteacher who has migrated to the USA.

Limestone constructs a vision of Barbados that encompasses suffering and achievement, heroic struggle and the setbacks of born of self-interest and timorous compromise. Above all, *Limestone* is never other than a poem: a vast treasure house of images, sounds and rhythms that move, entertain and absorb the reader in its world.

South Eastern Stages
ISBN: 9781845231989; pp. 66; pub. 2012; price: £8.99

Ranging from his native Barbados, across the Southern States (particularly Georgia, where he lives) and taking Caribbean perceptions to Brazil, journeying – by bus, by plane (and remembering earlier passages on the slave ship) – is seen as a truth of twenty-first century existence and a metaphor that is constantly refreshed by warmly empathetic observations of people at different stages in their passage through life. To travel with Kellman is to delight in his eye for the "polyphony in the common salt", the pleasures he finds even in the most casual of meetings, though he also knows that "nature's ears are kinder than men's". Whether in conversational free verse, or the regularities of his Tuk verse forms, Anthony Kellman's poetry engages with a felicity of phrase, surprising but apt comparisons and the musicality of his lines.